HIS RELUCTANT SUBMISSIVE

OWNED BOOK TWO

KL RAMSEY

PROLOGUE

AVALON

Avalon Michaels knew that being summoned to her father's house wasn't a good thing—it never was. She and her father tried to have as little to do with each other as possible, so being called to stop by at her earliest convenience made her nervous. Plus, she had consumed way too much coffee to be calm about anything.

She rang the bell which to most people might seem strange but it didn't feel right to just barge into her father's home anymore. She hadn't lived with him in some time and the familiarity of just waltzing into his home felt wrong. Surprisingly, her father answered the door himself and seemed downright chipper for a change.

"Ah, Avalon. I'm glad you could make it on such short notice," he said. "Come in." Ava did as he requested, filing past him and into the grand foyer. Every time she stepped foot into her childhood home, it made her a little sad. She thought about all the people who used to live there that were lost to her—her mother and brother. She hated how empty the big old house now seemed and she almost felt sorry for her father for having to live there alone. He must be haunted by the same ghosts as she was but he never let on.

"What's up, Dad? You said it was urgent so I'm here on my lunch break. I do need to be getting back to the office though," she lied. After meeting with her father, she really had no other plans for the day and hoped to head home early. There was a bubble bath and a glass of wine with her name all over them.

"This shouldn't take too long," he promised. "Can I get you anything?" He asked.

"Nope," she said. Ava made a show of checking her watch and her dad sighed and handed her a sealed envelope.

"What is this?" she asked. Ava hadn't received mail at her father's house in years.

"It's from the lawyers. I've been meaning to give this to you for a while now but I haven't seen you. My lawyer has been hounding me for weeks to get these to you and well, I guess time is running out," her father said. He wasn't making much sense but Ava tried to keep up.

"Time's running out for what?" she questioned.

"Until your birthday," he said. "It's a big one this year, right? The big three zero," he teased. Honestly, Ava wasn't sure what her birthday had to do with anything. Her father hadn't recognized her birthday in years.

Usually, she and Zara did something together to celebrate but that was about it. Her father hadn't called to wish her a happy birthday in years—why would he all the sudden be bringing it up?

"Well, go on, open it," he said. Ava cautiously did as she was told, carefully pulling the edges of the sealed envelope open as if she was afraid something was going to pop out at her.

When she finally got it open, she pulled free some papers that looked suspiciously like legal documents. "Will I need my lawyer to go over these?" she asked, still not sure what the papers were.

"There really isn't a need," her father said. "Everything is in order and completely legal, trust me. I'm sure you won't listen to me and you will have your lawyers combing through them despite my assurances." Her father was right; she didn't trust one word that came out of his mouth and if he expected her to sign some legal documents without having her lawyer look them over first, he was crazy.

She flipped through the papers and shoved them back into the envelope, deciding that she really didn't have the time or patience to read them over in her father's foyer. That's why she kept a lawyer on retainer.

"You're not even going to ask what they are?" her father asked. Ava could tell from his tone that he was disappointed.

"Like I said, I have to get back to work. I'm sure my lawyer will be able to clarify everything for me later," she offered. Ava turned to leave and her father growled in frustration. She didn't bother to turn around, knowing that if she did, he'd expect her to engage with him and that was the last thing she wanted. When her dad didn't get his way, he tended to get a little nasty and she didn't want to deal with that side of him.

"You won't be keeping the money your grandfather left you," he shouted after her. Ava stopped dead in her tracks. Her father hated that her grandfather had left her the majority of his fortune when he passed. She was closer to her grandfather than her father was and when the will was read and she walked away with most of the inheritance, her father refused to even speak to her. That went on for months, but ever since then he had been finding little ways to weasel back into her life.

"It's already a done deal, Dad. Grandpa left me almost everything and there isn't anything you can do about it."

His smile was mean and Ava knew she wasn't going to like what he had to say next. "There was a clause," he spat. "A marriage stipulation, if you will."

"What?" she questioned. "As in I have to be married to keep the money? How in the hell did you do that, Dad?" Ava accused.

"I didn't do anything except convince an old, dying man that it might be smart to ensure that his line of succession be in place. You want to keep your inheritance—you have to marry by your thirtieth birthday." Her father seemed almost pleased with himself and Ava knew that arguing with him would get her nowhere.

"Grandpa would have never willingly put that kind of stipulation on me," she said. "You had to have done something to convince him to do it."

"Either way, it's done. How much more time do you have until your special day?" He asked, already knowing full well that there were only two months until her birthday.

"Two months," she whispered.

"Well, you better get busy trying to find your better half then, my dear. Time is a wasting," he said.

"What happens if I don't get married by my thirtieth birthday?" she asked.

"That's the best part," he said. "It all goes to his next closest living heir—me." Ava didn't hide her gasp. The thought of her father getting all her grandfather's money made her sick. She knew for a fact it wasn't what her grandpa would have wanted either.

Ava couldn't stand there in that stuffy old house for a moment longer. She turned to leave and her father laughed. "In a hurry to leave, Ava?" he called after her.

"Yes," she said over her shoulder. She stopped at the front door and turned back to face him. "Like you said, Daddy, I have two months to find my better half. I better get cracking because there is no way I'm going to just let you walk away with grandpa's money." Ava noticed the subtle look of disapproval in her father's eyes and she knew she had hit a nerve with her empty threat. There was really no way to keep him from getting his hands on her inheritance because finding a man and convincing him to marry her in two months, was going to prove damn near impossible.

Two Weeks Later

Avalon sat in the corner of the club and watched the couples and a few threesomes who had gathered around the room. She thought about running out of there as quickly as possible, but the thought of not facing Corbin's stupid dare head on made her feel like a coward.

She spied him as soon as he walked into the BDSM club and wasn't sure if she was worried he'd see her or if he'd find someone else more interesting and forget all about her. Corbin Eklund was a tease and she'd do well to remember that before she lost her heart to the serial player. She watched him for a few minutes and could tell the exact moment he saw her. His sexy smirk told her all she needed to know—he didn't believe she would actually take him up on his bet to show up at the club. He made his way across the crowded club and towered over her.

"I didn't think you'd show, Darlin'," he drawled. "What made you decide to go through with it?" Ava smiled up at him, trying not to let on what the little nickname he called her did to her girl parts. Every damn time he called her Darlin', she had to bite back her moan. Frankly, everything Corbin did made her a little crazy but telling him that could never happen. He had asked her to the club because he thought she wouldn't take him up on his bet and then she'd lose at the little game they had been playing. Losing wasn't an option for her. Ava was competitive but losing to Corbin Eklund felt worse than forfeiting to the devil himself.

He was the sexiest devil she had ever met but keeping that to herself was for the best. The man already had a serious problem with humility—he had none. He was the most confident, self-possessed, arrogant man she'd ever met and for some reason, that wasn't enough for Ava to stay away from him.

"Well, a bet is a bet—so here I am. Now what are you planning on doing with me, Corbin?" she asked. Honestly, she tried not to think about the possibilities leading up to tonight. She had two very long nights to think about what she wanted him to do to her. Ava had spent the past two nights restlessly tossing and turning trying to figure out how to get through this evening with her heart intact and the answer wasn't one she easily entertained—she wouldn't.

She had met Corbin a few months prior, when her best friend, Zara hooked up with Corbin's best friend, Aiden. They stood up for their friends at their quicky wedding a few months ago, when they got married. She was happy for her friend; Zara deserved every happiness she had found with Aiden and his two little girls. But now, Ava felt more alone than ever. It wasn't as if Zara was moving away but being the new Senator's wife was going to take up a good deal of her time. Well, that and the fact she was a new step-mother to two of the cutest little girls Ava had ever seen and Zara was pregnant with her first baby. There would be little to no time for the two of them to hang out or stay up all night talking about life and guys. Those days were over and it was time for Ava to grow up and move on.

He smiled down at her and winked. Ava rolled her

eyes at just how cheesy he was but she smiled back at him. She couldn't help it—his carefree nature was infectious. She needed to relax and just enjoy tonight because it had been a damn long time since she had any fun with a man. Hell, she lost count of how many months it had been since she had sex. This night was about finding her mojo and getting back in the saddle again, nothing more. Corbin had made her no promises and she wouldn't ask for any.

"I have no idea what to do with you, Avalon," he admitted. "You showing up here caught me completely off guard."

Her smile turned quickly into a frown at his admission. She stood from her seat. "Hey, if this wasn't something you wanted to happen, I can just leave. No hard feelings or anything," she sassed. Ava turned to leave and Corbin caught her by the arm.

"Stop," he commanded.

"Really Corbin, it's fine if you aren't interested," she said. Actually, it hurt like hell knowing he didn't want her, but she wasn't going to stand in that damn club and cry all over him. She was stronger than that and sobbing all over a guy just wasn't her scene.

"Who the fuck says I don't want you, Darlin'?" he asked. He took her hand and led it to his bulging erection, letting her feel every impressive inch of his arousal. "Does this feel like I don't want you?" Ava let her shaking fingers aimlessly run over his shaft and he groaned and leaned into her touch.

He watched her; a hungry look in his eyes and she knew he was going to give her exactly what she had been needing. She tried for coy, even asking, "Is that all for me?" but Corbin didn't seem to be buying her blasé question.

"Don't play with me, Ava," he whispered. "I've wanted this for too long." Hearing him admit he wanted her did strange things to her girl parts. She felt a new wetness coat her lacy panties and she was sure one touch from Corbin would set her off.

"How long, Corbin?" she almost whispered. Ava cleared her throat, "How long have you wanted me?" she questioned.

Corbin looked her up and down, as if taking in every inch of her curvy body. "I've wanted you since the first night I saw you—at Aiden's place the day the news story broke about him and Zara. You were so fucking beautiful and the way you fiercely stuck up for your friend made me hot." She had no idea Corbin even noticed her that night. She thought back to their trip to take the girls for ice cream and then the park, and as far as she knew, Corbin found her annoying more than anything. Boy, had she misread the situation.

"Wow," Ava whispered.

"Yeah, wow," Corbin confirmed. "So, now that we've cleared that up, I'll ask again. What made you decide to accept my little bet and show up here?" Corbin had finally come clean with her and now it was her turn to give him some truths. She wasn't a coward but Ava knew telling him she wanted him just as much was going to sting a little. She had spent months trying to act nonchalant about anything having to do with the big guy but seeing him now, towering over her, made Ava want to take a chance.

She went up on her tiptoes and brushed back a strand of Corbin's overly long, dark hair back from his eyes. He had the most soulful brown eyes she had ever seen. Whenever he looked at her she felt as if he could see straight into her soul. "I showed up here tonight for the same reason you did, Corbin. I want you just as much as you want me. I won't lie about that or hide behind my own insecurities."

Corbin wrapped an arm around her waist and pulled her up his body, kissing his way into her mouth. God, he tasted like bottled sunshine and she couldn't seem to get enough of him. "Thank fuck," he whispered against her lips. She wrapped her legs around his waist and he walked back to the hallway that led from the public playroom to the private rooms for exclusive members. She had only been to the club a handful of times before but Ava remembered her way around.

He opened a door and walked in, setting her on the bed that took up most of the room. "This is my private room," he said. "I thought we could do a quiet setting tonight, unless you would like to try the playroom," he offered. Ava didn't want to get into the fact she had been a guest at the club before accepting his dare tonight. Truthfully, she loved the kinky lifestyle and was training to be a sub, but telling Corbin that didn't exactly feel like "first date" material.

"This works for me," she admitted, sitting back on the bed. She didn't hide the fact she was checking Corbin out, looking his body up and down. She loved that he was dressed like a total badass tonight. Usually, he was impeccably dressed in a suit. Ava guessed that matched his whole CEO business owner day gig but tonight he was dressed to fit who he really was. Corbin filled out his black tee, showing off all his muscles and his full sleeves of tattoos. She knew he had quite a few of them hiding under his dress shirt but not full sleeves. And the way his erection pressed against his jeans almost looked painful.

"You keep looking at me like that, Darlin' and this won't last very long," he growled.

"Sorry," she said. "I was just trying to figure out just how far up your tattoos go." Corbin gave her a wolfish grin and she knew she was in trouble.

"Well, I can help you figure that out, honey," he said, yanking his black t shirt up over his head. She gasped when he revealed most of his upper torso was covered in tats. She had always thought Corbin was hot, but seeing him in only his jeans, she realized he was down-right beautiful.

"Corbin," she whispered. It was all Ava could manage because he literally took her breath away.

CORBIN

He watched Avalon as she looked over his upper body and when she whispered his name, all Corbin could think about was getting inside of her. He wanted her more than he wanted his next breath, but he also knew this might be his only shot with her and he needed to take his time. Tonight was a fluke, a bet he thought he was going to lose but instead he had won the woman he was dreaming about for months now. Avalon Michaels hadn't agreed to be his, but gifting him with one night of her time was more than he could have ever hoped for.

After they all returned from Aiden and Zara's honeymoon, he convinced Ava to go out for a drink with him. At first, she protested, saying she was already behind at work and making some excuse about having to get caught up with laundry. Just when he thought she was going to walk away from him, she turned back and agreed to just one drink.

He took her to his favorite little bar that had live

music loud enough they had to sit incredibly close to each other just to have a conversation. One drink turned into three and then four and before he knew it, they were both drunk and he was betting her she wouldn't go to the BDSM club where he was a member. It was the same club where Aiden met Zara, so he was hoping lightning would strike twice and somehow Ava would end up in his bed.

The next day he texted her reminding Ava about the dare she boldly accepted with the help of alcohol. He was sure her return text would tell him to go fuck himself but she didn't. Instead, she confirmed she would be at the club at nine sharp and even told him not to be late. Like he would show up even a second past nine and chance her leaving. Corbin had waited too long for something like this to fall into his lap with Ava. He wasn't about to fuck it up.

Now, they were finally in his private room and he was wondering just how much kink Avalon would allow. They really never discussed sexual likes and dislikes and this was uncharted territory for him. As a Dom, he knew communication was key and neither of them would get what they needed if he didn't ask questions. Still, he worried asking Avalon what she liked in bed was going to send her running from his room and that was the last thing he wanted.

"Hey," she said, kneeling on the bed in front of him. "Where did you just go?" she questioned. Knowing Ava knew him well enough to pick up on the fact he was worried about this next part did crazy things to his heart. She ran her hands down his face and he pulled

14

them back up to his mouth to gently kiss her fingers and then let them rest on his chest. He liked the way she flexed them into his flesh, as if she already needed more from him, and they hadn't even gotten started yet.

"I was trying to decide how to ask you what you like—you know in bed," he said. She giggled and he took a step back from her, letting her hands fall back to her side. "That wasn't quite the response I was hoping for, Avalon," he said.

"No Corbin, I'm sorry," she said, reaching for him. "I was just laughing because I was worried about telling you what I like—you know kink wise," she admitted. He took a deep breath and stepped back towards her.

"What kind of kink do you like, Avalon?" he asked. She gasped when he ran his hands through her short dark hair, grabbing a handful and giving it a yank, forcing her to look up at him. She moaned and closed her eyes, telling him she liked it a little rough.

"Eyes open, Darlin'," he commanded. Ava did exactly as he asked and he knew she was going to be a perfect sub. "You've done this before, haven't you honey?" he questioned. She shyly nodded her answer.

"I'm going to need more than head nods, Ava. Give me the words," he demanded. He knew he could be a little overbearing, but Avalon seemed to take everything he was throwing at her and giving him back everything in return.

"Yes, Corbin," she hissed when he tightened his grip on her hair.

"Sir," he corrected. "In here, you will call me Sir."

Avalon smiled up at him, "Yes, Sir," she corrected. "I

have done this before. I've had training to be a sub, here at the club." The thought of any other Dom taking Ava on as a sub made his inner caveman roar to life and he was pissed. There was nothing he could do about the past but if another Dom tried to touch her, he'd break the guy in two.

"How long ago?" he questioned. He knew he was torturing himself with the details of her time at the club but he couldn't help it. Corbin needed to know before he moved forward with her.

"About a year ago, I wanted to explore this life—you know see if it was for me." He released her hair and sat down on the bed next to her. Corbin pulled Ava's small body onto his lap, loving the way she so eagerly straddled him.

"Is it?" he whispered, "the life for you?" She framed his face with her small hands again and loved the way she seemed to need to touch him.

"Yes, Sir," she whispered against his lips.

He let out his pent- up breath, not realizing he had been holding it, waiting for her answer. "I'm so fucking happy to hear you say that, Ava," he admitted.

"I take it you like it kinky then too?" she asked.

"I do," he said. "I'm a Dom and God, I've dreamed of what I want to do to you, Darlin'," he said. Corbin rolled Ava under his body and pressed her into the mattress. "You're going to need a safe word, Avalon," he ordered. "I plan on taking you to the very edge of your limits and since this is our first time together, I want to be sure you are with me."

Ava smiled up at him and seemed to think for a

minute. "Ice cream," she whispered. "For the first time we met," she said.

He kissed his way into her mouth, loving the breathy little sighs and moans she gave him. He wasn't sure how he had gotten so lucky but he really didn't want to think about that right now. All Corbin wanted to do was concentrate on making Avalon his. The rest of his worries could wait until tomorrow. She hadn't made him any promises beyond the here and now and he planned on soaking up every second with her.

AVALON

"Ice cream it is then," Corbin growled. "I'm going to push you to your limits, Darlin'." Ava nodded, wanting to let him know she was with him. She knew how important communication was within the Dom/sub relationship from her training.

"Yes, Sir. I want that too, please," she smiled up at him.

"If you use your safe word, this all stops and we can talk about what you didn't like," Corbin said. Ava nodded again and Corbin gave a sharp yank to her short hair. "The words, baby," he ordered.

"I understand," she said, dramatically rolling her eyes. "I'm with you, Corbin—completely," she sassed. Corbin's expression turned from turned on to pissed in a matter of seconds.

"I'm not playing games here, Ava. I just told you that I've waited too long for you to not take this seriously. If you don't feel the same, just tell me now and we can forget this ever happened," he threatened. Ava instantly regretted her sass. She knew better than to be a brat but she was a work in progress when it came to being a submissive. She wanted to at least try to give Corbin what he was asking for; otherwise she might never get another chance with him.

"I'm sorry, Corbin. I suck at this submissive thing sometimes. I will try to do better—I promise," she swore, crossing her heart with her hand for good measure. She almost forgot that she still had her clothes on until her fingers lightly brushed her t-shirt causing her nipple to pucker from the sensation. Judging by the way Corbin looked her over, he noticed the same thing.

"Sir," he whispered into her ear. Corbin grabbed the hem of her white t-shirt that barely covered her belly and tugged it up over her head. Ava obligingly lifted both arms, letting him pull her shirt from her body, leaving her breasts completely bare for him.

How he expected her to follow their conversation now was a mystery. "Um, sorry?" she questioned. Corbin's eyes flared with need as he looked over her body.

"I'm sorry, Sir," he said correcting her. "You called me by my name and that isn't what we are doing here tonight, Ava. You are my submissive for the night and if you want to address me, you will call me Sir," Corbin ordered.

Ava didn't hide her smile, "Yes, Sir," she hissed the last word, adding emphasis to show Corbin she was capable of playing things his way. Corbin stood, shaking his head at her; his smile playing with his lips as if he was amused by Ava's sassy spirit. When he took a step back and crossed his arms over his massive tattooed chest, it was her turn to ogle him.

"I hear you saying the correct words, Darlin' but I'm not sure you mean them. You are a brat, Ava," he said.

"I've been told," she sassed. When Corbin stood at his full height in all his angry glory, he was quite a sight. Most people would be intimidated by just his size alone, but Ava was taught the bigger they were, the harder they fell, by her grandfather. She was never the type of person to back down from a challenge and now was no different.

Ava crossed her arms over her own bare chest and Corbin let his eyes dip to follow her movement. She knew that standing her ground might land her in some trouble with the big Dom, but she was curious to see just how far he'd let her push him. Plus, she had a sneaky feeling that Corbin would end up punishing her and the thought of that made her pussy wet. Ava squeezed her thighs together, trying to hide the fact that she was wet and ready for him. Her short schoolgirl skirt barely covered her ample ass and she worried that Corbin would be able to see her arousal.

"I think you could use a few reminder lessons, Ava," he said. "For one, I'd like to teach you to control that sassy mouth of yours and then we can move onto your fidgeting," he said. She knew he was trying to go for threatening and maybe even a little menacing, judging by his tone, but all Ava could hear were the promises he was making her.

"Yes Sir," she whispered.

"On your knees, Darlin," he drawled. Ava felt downright giddy at his command and she immediately sunk to her knees. "Thank you, Avalon," he said. His gravely tone gave him away and Ava could tell that Corbin was on edge. He was just as turned on by this whole scene as she was. She licked her lips and looked up at him through her lashes, using every trick she was taught last year about pleasing her Dom. Corbin moaned as he unzipped his pants and let his cock spring free.

Avalon's breath hitched and he smiled down at her, even giving her a saucy wink. She watched as Corbin pulled his pants off and tossed them in the corner of the room. He liked showing off for her, palming his own cock to let her know exactly what he was going to give her.

"You're big, Sir," she whispered. Corbin's chuckle resonated through the room and she worried that whatever he planned next might have her safe word out of her mouth before they even got started.

"Ready?" He looked her over and she wasn't sure how to answer his question. Was she ready for Corbin Eklund to make her his—hell yeah! But would she be able to take all of him and his dominance? She wished she could enthusiastically answer the same to that question but she wasn't sure that she'd be able to.

"Yes," she stuttered, "Sir, I believe I'm ready."

"Let's talk about what you like and don't like. If you haven't done something I'm asking you to do, then just speak up," he offered.

"Okay, Sir," she agreed.

"So, I'm guessing that you have had sex before?" Corbin started. Ava giggled and nodded.

"Yes, I've had sex before, Sir," she said.

"Well, I had to ask. We wouldn't want a fuck up like Aiden and Zara had, would we?" Ava thought back over the past few months and the roller coaster that her best friend, Zara, seemed to be on. When Ava dared Zara to go to the BDSM club, she met Aiden and lied about her virginity. Well, Zara didn't exactly lie about it, but she didn't come right out and share that she was a virgin. Aiden and Zara seemed to find a way forward though and Ava had to admit she was happy for her best friend.

"No, that wouldn't be good," she agreed.

"Anal?" Corbin asked.

"I've had it a few times but I can't say I'm a huge fan of anal, Sir," she offered.

"Well, maybe your partner didn't know what he was doing," Corbin teased. He took a step toward her and stood so close she could smell his sexy, musky scent mixed with his cologne. He always smelled like heaven and now was no exception. She wanted to lean forward and suck the head of his cock into her mouth but she waited. Instead, she watched as Corbin stroked his hard shaft, making her mouth water.

"For the rest of these questions, I want you to hum if you have done what I'm asking or if you'd like to try it. Understand?" She must have looked at him like he was crazy and Corbin laughed.

"Why do I need to hum? Can't I just say yes or no?" she questioned.

"It's going to be hard to form words from this point on, since I plan on having my cock shoved down that pretty throat of yours, Darlin'." Ava gifted him with her sly smile and nodded. She opened her mouth, as if offering him what he wanted and he rested the tip of his cock on her bottom lip. "Take as much of me as you can, Ava," he ordered.

Really it was no easy feat to take all of Corbin, but she managed to take most of him, greedily sucking him to the back of her throat and swallowing around his massive shaft.

"Fuck, baby," he hissed. "When you do that, I can't thing straight." Ava felt her inner goddess spring to life with Corbin's praise and she knew she'd give him anything he wanted.

Corbin ran a hand down her cheek and Ava looked up at him. It was such a soft, caring gesture; it almost threw her off guard. "You are so fucking beautiful, Avalon," he whispered. Ava moaned and sucked him to the back of her throat again. If she wasn't careful, she was going to forget that Corbin wanted her for just one night. This wasn't a date or even leading to the possibility of one. This was sex between a Dom and a submissive. She wasn't his and never would be. It wasn't the way Corbin worked.

Ava knew guys like Corbin—hell, she only dated guys like him. It was easier that way. She didn't want a messy relationship that got in the way of her work commitments and personal goals. Ava had so much she wanted to do in life and none of it involved feelings, a boyfriend or falling in love. All that mushy shit would have to wait until later.

Avalon concentrated on sucking Corbin in and out of her mouth. That was easy—sex could help her forget the things that she told herself she wasn't ready for because when Corbin looked at her the way he was, she was ready to throw all her personal plans out the window and agree to anything he wanted from her.

"How about spanking?" he questioned, bringing her thoughts back to the present. Ava hummed her approval around his cock, feeling her own arousal coating her thighs. Every time Corbin offered another kinky activity, she felt a new surge of wetness between her legs.

"Will you let me tie you up?" Corbin asked, shoving his cock to the back of her throat. She once again hummed and Corbin moaned. She knew he was close but she didn't want to push him.

"Flogging and other forms of spanking punishments?" He questioned. Avalon hummed and Corbin pumped in and out of her mouth.

"Blindfold, nipple clamps, sex toys, rope play?" He listed them all off and Ava had to admit they all sounded like things she would enjoy. She hummed her agreement.

"Will you let me share you with another man?" He asked. Ava didn't make a sound, not sure how she felt about that idea. Would she want to let Corbin give her to another Dom to use? A part of her thought it was hot, but there was a little voice inside of her that was telling her that if he could share her so easily, she must not be worth much. Plus, if she only had tonight with him, she wanted Corbin all to herself.

Corbin pulled free from her mouth, causing Ava to mewl in protest. He chuckled, "Sorry, Darlin'." He said. "I don't want to finish in your sexy mouth. I want in

24

that pussy of yours but first we need to talk about my last question."

Ava shrugged. "I'm not sure I'd like to be shared," she admitted. "I only have you for tonight and I don't want to waste any time," she said, giving him an honest answer.

Corbin pulled her up his body, from her kneeling position, to stand in front of him. Ava looked down at her bare feet and Corbin crooked a finger under her chin, raising her face to look at him. "What if I wanted this to be more than just one night?" he asked.

Ava shook her head. "I don't know if I'd be able to give you more," she admitted. "I didn't say anything earlier, but I'm leaving tomorrow for France and I don't know when I'll be back."

Corbin dropped his hand from her chin. "Why didn't you say so before now?" Corbin grumbled.

"Because it wouldn't have mattered. We agreed to one night, Corbin. I have to go on a business trip. I'm sure your company requires you to leave town and you don't tell everyone else your business," she said.

"No, you're right. And, we did say that this was a one night deal. Fine, no sharing," he said. Ava could tell that he was trying to change the subject and she had to admit she was thankful he did. "Any other hard limits?" he asked.

"I don't like electric or fire play," she admitted. Ava tried to remember her training and all the different things she had to experience as a submissive. "I think that about covers it though," she said.

Corbin nodded, "Noted," he said. Ava could tell that

25

he was shorter with her and she worried that telling him about her trip might have been a mistake. Really, she didn't think it was a big deal but judging from Corbin's sour mood, it was.

He crossed the room to sit on the bed. "Come here," he ordered, patting his bare legs. His cock jetted out from between his legs and Ava hoped that the talking portion of their evening was just about over. She stood in front of Corbin as if waiting for further instruction. "I'm going to spank your ass red and then I'm going to tie you up and fuck you until you can't remember your name."

"Yes Sir," she said.

"Good girl," he praised. "Lay over my lap with your ass up for me, Darlin'," he ordered. Ava did as asked and when he landed the first blow without warning, she yelped.

"This is going to go fast and hard, Ava," he said. "If it's too much for you, use your safe word." It almost sounded like he was issuing her a dare. She knew that she had pissed him off and Ava worried that he'd try to push her to use her safe word. She loved a good challenge and from his tone, Corbin was issuing her one.

"Am I being punished, Sir?" she asked.

Corbin didn't answer, just rubbed his big palm over her ass where the first smack probably left a welt. When more than a few minutes passed, she turned to her side to look back at him.

"Corbin?" She asked. He turned away from her, so she couldn't see his expression and Ava knew that something was wrong. "Please tell me if I did something wrong," she begged.

"No," he breathed. "I'm mad at myself for letting this get so out of hand. I am mad and I can't do this—not now. I wouldn't ever touch you while I'm angry with you, Ava."

"What did I do to make you so upset?" she asked, standing from his lap. She righted her skirt and sat down on the bed next to him. "Please talk to me, Corbin," she asked.

"I'm mad that you are going to France and didn't tell me. But I'm mainly angry at myself because you are right—it's none of my business. I guess I was just hoping for more with you, Ava and I was too much of a chicken to ask."

Hearing that Corbin wanted more with her did crazy things to her heart. She just wasn't ready to give him more of herself. Her company was sending her to France for a few weeks to do some buying. She was a fashion acquisitions manager for a major department store in town and part owner in a clothing design company. They wanted her to stay in Europe until she was finished and Ava had no idea when she'd be back in town. Honestly, she needed some time away from home and her family. She had seen her father earlier that week and he had dropped a bomb that had an expiration date ticking down on it. Ava needed some time away to think over what her next step would be. Dealing with her father was always like that, playing a game of chess and she had to carefully consider her next move or chance losing the game to him and losing wasn't something she liked to do. Being sent to France could not have come at a better time, even if the sexiest man she had ever seen wanted her to stick around.

"I'm sorry that I didn't tell you sooner, Corbin. Maybe we can pick this up when I get back to town?" she asked.

Corbin gifted her with his shy, sexy smile. "I'd like that, Ava," he said. Ava decided to take a chance, straddling his lap, letting his cock slide through her slick folds.

"What's this?" Corbin asked, cocking an eyebrow at her.

"This is me trying to make peace with you. Forgive me?" Ava watched him, almost holding her breath waiting for him to answer.

"Yes," he whispered. Corbin kissed his way into her mouth, lifting her body from his lap and sliding her back down onto his cock. Ava moaned at the pleasure of being so full. He was big but they still fit and all she could think about was moving on him, riding him and giving them both all the pleasure they seemed to need. That was what she would concentrate on tonight— making Corbin remember every sinful detail of their time together and then when she got back to town, she'd give him another night. Maybe it was time to let a little romance into her busy schedule and Ava couldn't think of any other man she'd want to do that with more than Corbin Eklund.

CORBIN

Corbin had spent the better part of a week in meetings, putting out fires and feeling consumed by his memories of Avalon. She was everything he thought she would be and so much more. When he met Zara's sassy little friend, he couldn't work her out of his mind and he had tried. He spent countless nights at the club finding a sub to try to take his mind off Ava but nothing seemed to work. When she finally agreed to meet him at the club and give him one night, he wasn't sure if he was happy or upset about the whole deal. He was sure of one thing though, one night with Avalon wasn't enough and he worried he'd never be able to get her out of his mind.

After their night together, Avalon and he made each other the promise to make no promises. It was strange but he wanted so many fucking reassurances from her, but he wasn't ready to ask her for any of them. Ava made it clear that their night was just about sex and while she was away, she wouldn't fault him for enjoying the company of other subs at the club. He almost wanted to laugh in her face when she said it but he knew better than to piss her off. The thought of being with anyone else at the club made him cringe. He wanted one woman right now and she was thousands of miles away in France.

He asked her if the whole no promises thing was more for her, so she could see other men while she was away and Ava tried to assure him that she would be too busy to even notice another man. But, she never really gave him a straight answer and that really burned his ass.

"Hey," Aiden said, letting himself into Corbin's office. Aiden Bentley was his best friend and his business partner, but more than that he was like the brother Corbin never had.

"What's up?" Corbin asked, looking up from his computer screen.

"I haven't seen you around the office much this week. In fact, the only time I've seen your ugly mug was during meetings. Want to tell me what's going on with you?" Aiden said. He knew that his best friend could always tell when something was off with him and vice versa. They were a team and he'd expect no less from Aiden.

"It's a woman," Corbin said.

"Shit," Aiden cursed. "Please don't tell me this has anything to do with Avalon because if my wife finds out that you are screwing around with her best friend, she'll have my balls," Aiden grouched.

Corbin didn't hide his amusement. "Man, Zara already has your balls. I'm pretty sure she keeps them in a jar on her bedside table to remind you that she's in charge."

Aiden seemed to find the whole thing less funny than Corbin. Aiden was a Dom like him and he had found his perfect submissive in his new wife, Zara. Corbin often wondered if he'd ever find someone as perfect for him as Aiden had. Avalon was far from being a perfect submissive. In fact, the idea of her not giving him grief was a foreign one. Ava liked to question and give him sass around every corner and the thought of spanking her ass red for being a brat turned him completely on.

"Okay, I won't tell you about Ava and I spending a night together at the club and then the way she packed her shit and took off for France the next morning," Corbin complained.

"Dear God," Aiden growled. "Fuck, now I'm going to have to hear about how my best friend is fucking up Zara's best friend's life. I'll never hear the end of this."

"Calm down, man. I'm not fucking up anyone's life. I wanted more but Ava shot me down. She just left and made me promise that we'd make no promises," Corbin said.

"What the fuck does that even mean?" Aiden questioned.

"Hell if I know," Corbin grouched. "But all I can think about his Ava and some French asshole hooking up while I'm sitting here acting like a complete pussy about the whole thing," Corbin admitted.

"So, what are you going to do about it, man?" Aiden questioned.

"It's not that simple, Aiden," Corbin grouched.

"What's not simple? Do you want Ava?" Aiden asked.

"Yes," Corbin confirmed.

"All right—then what are you going to do about it?" Aiden asked again. Corbin paused. The last thing he needed was to dive into his feelings with his best friend. Aiden liked to jump in with both feet and not really think about the consequences. His friend always led with his heart and that wasn't who Corbin was. He was an over thinker, even a worrier and the idea of just jumping into the water feet first and to hell with the consequences, made him half crazy.

"I don't know, man. A part of me wants to have the jet fueled and go to France to set that woman straight and the other part of me wants to sit here and mope," Corbin grumbled. Aiden chuckled and Corbin knew he shot him a dirty look. He held up his hands as if in defense and took a step back from Corbin's desk.

"Sorry, man but if you want my two cents—" Aiden started.

"I don't," Corbin admitted.

Aiden chuckled again, "Well, I don't really give a fuck. I say call down to the runway and get the jet ready. Isn't that why we have all of this?" Aiden said motioning around Corbin's office. His friend wasn't wrong, although he'd never tell Aiden he was right. They had built a multi-million dollar company from nothing and they had a jet waiting to take them anywhere they pleased. What would it hurt to run to France and surprise Ava? He knew exactly what was holding him back, but saying the words out loud made him sound like a complete coward.

"What if she doesn't want me to chase after her? What happens if I get there and she tells me to get lost?" Corbin all but whispered his question.

Aiden sat down on one of the chairs that were in front of Corbin's massive desk. "I guess you'll never know how she'll react unless you get on that fucking plane and go find her. I'm betting I can get her address from Zara—just give it some thought." Corbin nodded and Aiden stood to leave his office.

"Thanks, man," Corbin called after him.

"Always," Aiden said and shut his office door. He knew he was being a coward, but the thought of flying halfway around the world only to be turned down, scared the shit out of him. He was usually so self-assured and confident when it came to women and what he wanted and didn't want. He usually just picked up subs at the BDSM club and played with them until he grew tired or found someone better to play with.

Ava was the first woman to make him feel things he had never felt before. She had him so twisted up inside he wasn't sure which end was up. Maybe it was time to put on his big boy pants and go to France to talk to Ava. What did he have to lose?

"Everything," Corbin whispered to himself, picking up his cell to call his pilot.

AVALON

Ava tried to bury herself in her job and it had worked for the most part, but she found France a great deal less interesting since having to leave Corbin's bed at the club. Thoughts of their night together consumed her waking hours and left her restless and needy all night long. All she wanted to do was cut her trip short and head back home but that wasn't who she was. Her boss would understand; hell, she owned a large percentage of the company so she could get away with just about anything. Ava knew better than the throw around her last name and money to get what she wanted though and living up to her boss's expectations was part of what drove her to stay put and finish her job there.

Her grandfather and father had both been heavily involved in local politics back home. They had both been popular Senators and she grew up very privileged. Some might say she was born with a silver spoon in her mouth, but she never wanted people to assume that she wasn't also a hard worker. Her family came from old money, but she didn't want to sit back on her inheritance and do nothing with her life. Ava decided at a very early age that she wanted to go into the fashion industry and after she got her Masters' in fashion design and marketing, she invested a good deal of money into a few of her favorite local designers. She liked the idea of helping a local struggling artist that might not have a chance without her money. She became friends with her current boss, Peter, and when he offered her forty-nine percent of his company and a job that she loved doing, she jumped at the chance. He was already established and honestly didn't really need her investment, but he liked what she was doing in the fashion community and made her the offer.

Now, with the possibility of losing her inheritance because of some crazy stipulation her father demanded her grandfather put into place, she was happy to have her little piece of the company to fall back on. That was also part of the reason why when Peter asked if she could go to France, she jumped at the chance. Ava needed to get away from town for a while and decide what to do about the little bomb her father dropped on her. He was all too happy to share the fact that he had convinced her grandfather to put a stipulation on the money she inherited from him. If she wasn't married by the age of thirty, she would lose everything—her townhouse, her car, her monthly allowance, bank accounts and assets—everything. Honestly, she was fine with having to make her own way, but when she found out that it would all revert to her dear old dad, she just about threw a tantrum. But, she wouldn't give him that satisfaction. Really, it would be playing right into her father's plans. She still had time—one and a half months to be exact and who knew what could happen in that time? Maybe she'd meet Mr. Right and he'd whisk her down the aisle and her father wouldn't get a penny of her money. Given that Corbin was her only prospect and the man seemed to be allergic to even the word "commitment", she was going to have to make some hard and fast decisions. The first being where she was going to live once she got back home. The second would be what the hell to do about Corbin Eklund.

Ava decided to call back home and check on everyone and if Corbin's name casually came up, she wouldn't mind. She picked up her cell and called her best friend Zara, hoping she'd be willing to listen and give her some advice.

"Hey, girl," she said, trying for casual.

"Don't 'hey girl' me, Avalon Michaels," Zara spat into the other end of the phone call. Her friend was very pregnant and Ava wasn't ever sure which person she was going to get when she called—her nice best friend or "I'm ready to murder someone" Zara. Tonight, she apparently was talking to the latter.

"Okay, what is going on now?" Ava asked.

"You are going on," Zara said. "You went to the club with Corbin and didn't tell me?" Ava sighed into the phone. She knew that sooner or later word would get around and if she had to guess, Corbin had talked to Aiden and now the cat was out of the bag.

"Corbin told Aiden?" She knew she was asking a question but honestly, she already knew the answer.

"Yes!" Zara's temper was sounding more heated by the minute. "Care to explain to me why I had to hear the news from my husband and not my best friend who may or may not be my daughter's Godmother now?"

"Hey, you can't hold my Godmother status over me like that. Either I'm in or I'm out but don't use my Goddaughter against me like that, Z," Ava ordered.

There was a pause on the other end of the line and Ava worried that she had lost the call. Zara sobbed into the other end and she instantly regretted her words. "Aww, Z," she crooned. "Don't cry."

"I can't help it," Zara cried. "I'm hormonal." Ava wasn't sure what to do or say. She wasn't a crier and having a best friend that currently cried over everything wasn't a picnic.

"Listen, if you'd rather I call later—" Ava started.

"No," Zara sniffled. "I'll get it together, I promise," she swore. "So, why are you calling me all the way from France? Isn't it the middle of the night there?" Zara was right—it was two in the morning, not that it mattered since she couldn't sleep.

"Yeah, I guess my body and brain are still on home time." Ava suddenly felt like a complete chicken. The last thing she wanted to do was involve her pregnant best friend in her problems but she really had no one else to turn to. "Listen, I'll call you another time and we can talk," Ava offered.

"I'm assuming you called me to ask about him?" Zara taunted. There would be no lying to her. Zara seemed to know her inside and out and not being completely honest went against their strict girl code.

"Yeah," Ava admitted. "What do I do about him?"

"Well, I'm assuming that you like him. You know like him, like him." Ava rolled her eyes and giggled.

"Are we back in middle school, Z?" she questioned.

"No," Zara defended. "I'm just trying to get a feel of where the two of you stand since this was the first I've heard of you liking him—you know directly from the horse's mouth." Ava winced at Zara's slight.

"Please don't call me a horse, Z," Ava teased. "And God help me, I like him, like him. I just have no clue what to do about it."

"You're going to have to make a decision fast," Zara said. "He took the jet and rumor has it he's heading for France."

"What?" Ava questioned.

"Yep," Zara confirmed.

"Why the hell didn't you call to tell me this earlier?" Ava sounded as panicked as she currently felt. "When will he get here? Oh my God, what do I wear or say or even do?"

Zara's laughter filled the other end of the line. "Yeah, this sounds exactly like middle school," she teased. "I'm sure you'll figure it all out. You might want to hurry though. He left yesterday."

"Fuck," Ava swore. Zara giggled and ended the call. Ava looked at her phone as if it somehow personally offended her and thought about throwing the damn thing across the room. She let an angry growl rip from her chest and looked around her hotel room in a panic.

"What the hell do I do now?" She shouted into the air, half expecting someone to answer her. Really, there was only one thing to do—run. She'd find another hotel or at least change rooms. Avoiding Corbin was her only hope for eventually forgetting him. Until she could figure out her shit, that was her only option.

Ava grabbed her suitcase, shoving everything she had brought with her into it, not taking the time to neatly pack her things as she usually did. She found her purse and her jacket and did one last check of her room before heading out. Ava pulled her door shut and headed to the elevators, jamming her thumb into the lit button as if that would help it ascend any faster.

She breathed a sigh of relief when her floor number lit up above the elevator doors and tried to patiently wait while the doors opened. The ding of the elevator doors gave her a sense of relief that she hadn't had in days and when the doors slowly opened to reveal the sexy Dom standing on the other side, her heart sank.

Corbin smiled at her and stepped off the elevator and practically bumped into her allowing others to exit. "Ava," he whispered.

"Why are you here?" she asked. She looked up his big body and made the mistake of looking him in the eyes. Corbin's expressions always gave him away and the sadness and confusion she saw in his eyes was nearly her undoing.

"I came to find you," he admitted. "Were you leaving?" he asked.

"No," she said. He looked down at the suitcase in her hand and back up at her, his sexy smirk firmly in place. "Well, not now," she admitted.

"Let me guess—you talked to Z and she told you I

was on my way to find you and you panicked. You do know I have the resources to find you, even in a city this size, right?" He looked her up and down again and Zara could feel her blush. What was it about this man that made her act like a giddy schoolgirl at prom?

"And you know that I have the resources to never be found again—by anyone, right?" Ava didn't usually flaunt her money but she wouldn't let Corbin's wealth intimidate her. She could probably match him dollar for dollar if he wanted to go toe-to-toe with her.

Corbin sighed and put his hands on his hips. "This isn't going like I planned," he admitted.

"What was the plan here, Corbin?" Ava waited him out. She wasn't sure if she wanted to tell him to go the fuck away or jump into his arms and tell him to take her.

"I was hoping that we could talk," he said.

Ava's laugh sounded more like a cackle and she turned to walk back to her room. There would be no running or hiding now, so she might as well kick off her heels and drop her belongings if she was going to have to a come to Jesus meeting with the sexy alpha who was currently staring her down. She looked back over her shoulder to where Corbin seemed frozen to his spot.

"You coming or not?" she asked.

"Yeah," Corbin said, chasing after her to keep up.

Ava opened her door and tossed her bags in the corner of the room. She took off her heels and put them by the door and pulled off her jacket. Ava could feel Corbin's eyes on her, watching her as if he was just as clueless in all of this as she was.

"Make yourself at home," she offered. "The mini bar is in the other room and I'll be in soon. I just need to change." Corbin nodded and found his way into the adjoining sitting room. She could hear him rummaging through her bar as she opened her suitcase to find her pajamas. She was going to be comfortable while dealing with Corbin—she owed herself at least that. She found her favorite set; the ones covered in polar bears and went into her bathroom to change. By the time she had found her way to the sitting room, Corbin was lounging on her settee, a drink in his hand and another for her waiting on the table in front of him.

"I thought you might like a drink," he said, motioning to where her glass sat on the coffee table. "Rum and pineapple juice, right?" he asked. She was surprised he remembered her drink order from their one night together. She nodded, taking the drink and sitting across the room from him, giving herself some much needed space.

"Cute pajamas," Corbin teased.

"Thanks," Ava said, taking a sip of her drink. So, what would you like to talk about?" she asked. Ava knew she sounded like a bitch but she was tired and confused. The man she couldn't stop thinking about over the past week was finally sitting in front of her. She was confused and worried that she would assume or say the wrong thing, so letting Corbin get his story out first seemed like a good enough plan.

"I missed you, Ava," he said. "I know you wanted to keep things between us casual, but I don't know if that's an option for me," he admitted. Ava could feel her heart beating and worried that Corbin would be able to hear it across the small space that separated the two of them.

"Tell me you missed me, Ava," he ordered. "Fuck, tell me I'm not a complete lunatic for coming all this way to track you down."

Ava took another sip of her drink, not sure what to say. He was telling her everything she wanted to hear, but she also knew the truth about Corbin—he was not a man who dated. He met women at the club and he fucked. She knew from just their one night together that wasn't going to be enough for her. God help her, she wanted more than that from him and Ava knew she couldn't expect him to be able to give her that.

"I missed you too, Corbin," she admitted. "But, I don't see how this thing between us will work out. I know you well enough to know you don't date. I don't want to be a fuck buddy, so that leaves us at a bypass in our relationship. I'd rather end things then jeopardize our friendship. It would kill Z and Aiden if we couldn't be in the same room together. It wouldn't be fair to do that to them. This way, we can part ways and still remain friends."

"I don't want to be friends," Corbin growled. "I don't want to be your fuck buddy, as you so colorfully called what is happening between the two of us. I want you, Ava. Is it so hard to believe that I may have changed and am looking for something more than just casual hookups at the club?"

Ava looked him over and every part of her wanted to believe him—except her heart. She worried that if she trusted what he was telling her, she'd end up losing that to him and there might not be any coming back from that.

Ava set her drink down and covered her face with her hands. "Fuck, don't cry," Corbin soothed. Ava pulled her hands free from her face and looked over at him. She almost wanted to laugh at the concern she saw etched in his brown eyes.

"I'm not crying," she corrected. "In fact, I rarely cry—just for future reference."

Corbin sat back and crossed his ankle over his knee, "Good to know, Darlin'." He smiled at her and winked; his mask firmly back in place. This was the Corbin she knew—not the kind, caring man who worried about making her cry. This Corbin was the big, badass Dom who told her what to do and expected her to do it. This was the Corbin she understood.

"Listen, I'm tired and I have a long day ahead of me tomorrow. How about you get back on your plane and go home and we can catch up and chat once I get back?" She stood, effectively dismissing him but he didn't seem to take the hint.

"I thought you might say that but you see, I don't do well with other people giving me orders," he said, standing to tower over her. "How about this—I'll let you get some sleep and you let me take you to dinner tomorrow night?"

"And how will you possibly take me to dinner if you are back home and I'm here in France?" she sassed.

Corbin set his drink down next to hers and pulled her against his body, not giving her any chance to object. "It will be possible because I'm staying in the room right next door to you, baby." Corbin crushed his lips against hers, taking what he wanted and giving her no room for objections. It seemed to be his go- to move.

He broke the kiss leaving her breathless and a little off kilter. "Tell me you'll have dinner with me," he ordered.

"Yes," she breathed. Corbin released her, gave her a curt nod, and before Ava even knew what happened, was gone from her hotel room. He left her standing there confused and backtracking in her mind, trying to figure out what the hell just happened. If she was remembering the last few seconds correctly, she had just agreed to not only go to dinner with Corbin Eklund but to give him a chance to completely destroy her life and break her heart.

"Fuck," Ava whispered.

CORBIN

The next day, Corbin had woken before the sun, still trying to adapt to his jet lag. With all the traveling he did, he should be used to the time differences but he wasn't. Plus, he chalked up some of his insomnia to the fact that he couldn't wait for his date with Ava. He knew she was probably getting ready for work but he didn't want to check on her. He would just wait to see her tonight for their date. Besides, he had a lot of prep work to do if he was going to make it as magical as possible for Ava. He wanted to sweep her off her feet and convince Avalon to give him a chance and judging by her cold reception of him last night, he had his work cut out for him.

He had settled into the room next to Ava's and found where the staff had put his luggage. Last night hadn't gone exactly how he planned but he was counting it as a win. If he had his way, they would have ended up in one of their beds, but judging from the skepticism he saw every time he looked at Ava, she wouldn't allow that.

Getting her to agree to a date was a major victory for him and one that he wouldn't let fall flat. His first order of business would be to book the best table in town. He had a few favorite restaurants in France but one stuck out as the clear choice for their date. It was elegant and perfect, just like Ava and he was sure she'd love it.

Corbin would spend the day planning an unforgettable evening for Ava and then he'd talk her into spending the night with him. She had given him his chance and there was no way he was going to blow it again. This time, he'd do things the right way.

After spending the day making arrangements, he knocked on Ava's hotel door promptly at six, as she requested. She answered after his second knock and when she pulled the door open to reveal that she was in just a white fluffy bathrobe, he nearly swallowed his tongue.

"Um—you look hot, honey but I think you might be a little underdressed for dinner," he teased.

Ava smirked at him and ushered him into her room. "Well, I got stuck in an afternoon meeting that didn't feel like it was ever going to end. I decided to take a quick bath and then realized that I might have misjudged my time in the tub. Sorry," she offered. The thought of Ava naked and soaking in a tub full of bubbles had his cock springing to life and he wasn't sure he would be able to make it through the rest of the evening if she didn't put some clothes on fast. He silently pleaded with himself to remember that he didn't want to fuck up tonight and taking her to dinner and not just fucking her was a major part of his plan.

"I'll be ready in ten," she promised, grabbing her dress from her bed and sauntering off to the bathroom. She left the door open a crack and Corbin knew he was going to need a distraction in order to keep from peeking in on her.

"Take your time," he offered. "Our reservations aren't for another thirty minutes."

"Reservations?" she asked. "Wow, you've been busy today," she said. "By the way, the flowers you sent were lovely." Ava came out of the bathroom wearing a sapphire blue cocktail dress and she nearly took his breath away.

"You look gorgeous, honey," he said. Ava suddenly seemed nervous, smoothing her hands down her curves and he wished they were his hands feeling her every outline.

"Thanks," she said. "I picked this up today. I really wasn't planning on having many fancy dinners out while I was here. I have to admit, I was unprepared, but working in the fashion industry affords some luxuries."

"So, no special dinners out then?" he asked.

Ava shook her head. "No," she whispered. "Honestly, when I'm in France, it's all business. I don't have time for fancy dinners and usually just get room service and catch up on work." Hearing that Ava wasn't dating her way through the French male population as he feared while he was sitting back home, gave him hope.

Ava giggled, "You look as if you're relieved, Corbin," she teased.

"Well, it's just good to know that your whole stance on no promises didn't mean that you were running off to France to go out with other guys," he said.

"Is that what you thought? That I made that statement so I could come here and sleep with every man I met?" Her tone was teasing but Corbin could tell from the hint of anger that she was testing him.

"Yes and no," he admitted. "My imagination got the best of me and all I could think about was you with another man. Fuck, just that thought alone drove me insane, honey," he admitted. He wasn't sure if his honesty would earn him any points but he wouldn't give her anything less than the truth.

"I said what I did for your benefit, Corbin. I didn't want you to think that our one night together had me believing that you were making me any promises," she said. "I know the score—it was just one night and you like to hang out at the club. I said that we would make each other no promises for your benefit, not mine." He nodded and took a step towards her, wanting to close some of the distance between them.

"You keep saying that you know the score, Ava but I'm not sure you do. What if I want to make you some promises?" he asked. She looked him up and down, silently questioning him. Corbin knew he was throwing a wrench in their "keep it casual" mantra, but he just didn't care anymore. It was time he laid all his cards on the table and let Avalon know just where he stood.

Ava looked just as nervous about their little date as

he felt. Honestly, this was all new to him—taking a woman out to dinner and having to make conversation.

"So," Ava stuttered. Corbin reached down to take her hand into his, trying to help steady her nerves.

"So," he whispered back. "You don't have to be nervous, Ava. It's just me," he offered.

"I know but this is starting to feel suspiciously like a date and I am usually a bundle of nerves on a first date," she admitted.

"Well, I'm glad this feels like a date because that is exactly what I want it to be. I hope that's all right with you?" he said, waiting for her to give her agreement. Ava slowly nodded her head, her brown curls played in her eyes and he reached down to gently brush them back from her face. He liked the way Ava leaned into his touch, as if she craved it.

"As for the first date jitters; you can just forget them because this isn't our first date—not really," he said.

"You can't seriously consider the night in the club to be our first date. We didn't do much dating, as I recall," she teased.

"Nope," he said. He smiled at her and squeezed her hand into his. "Our first date was the first night we met —at Aiden's. As I recall, you went out to have ice cream with the girls and me." He remembered that night as if it was just yesterday. The news story leaked about Zara and Aiden and he met the most beautiful woman he had ever seen in his life—Ava. She took care of her best friend like a fierce mother hen and everything about her seemed to do it for him. If he remembered correctly, he was the one feeling like he had a million butterflies take up residence in his tummy and to say he was tongue-tied was an understatement. He forgot his own damn name every time Ava even looked in his direction. If he was being honest with himself, it was at that moment that his world started to spin off kilter and the only time it he felt any peace was when she was near.

"That doesn't count," she countered.

"It certainly does. I treated and you even shared that your favorite ice cream was chocolate chip. I think that definitely counts as a first date," he said.

"Why'd you wait so long to ask me on a second date then?" she asked. That was a good question. Their ice cream date happened months ago and so much had happened since, but that had nothing to do with his reason for not asking her out again.

"I was a coward," he admitted. "I was afraid you'd say no. Hell, the only way I got you to the club and into my bed was to basically dare you."

"Well, a bet is something I never renege on," she said. "I wouldn't have said no, by the way," she whispered. Corbin ran his thumb over her palm, eliciting a shiver from her.

"Thank you for telling me that, Ava," he said. "I'd like to get to know you a little better," he admitted.

Ava nodded, "Sure, I'm an open book. What would you like to know, Corbin?" He sat down on the side of her bed, trying for casual but kept a hold of her hand, needing their connection.

"Tell me about your family," he asked.

"What about our reservations?" she questioned.

"We have a little time," he lied, pulling her down to sit on his lap.

"Okay well, my grandfather was a Senator. In fact, Aiden now occupies his old Senate seat," she started.

"Yes, I'm aware," Corbin said. "I was sorry to hear about your grandfather's passing. It was all over the news. That must have been tough for you and your family, having it thrown in your face that way."

Ava shrugged, "Not really. I was taught that having power and money is nice but it comes with some draw-backs—like always being in the public eye. That's probably why I like traveling abroad so much. Here, no one really knows my family and I'm free to just be me. That must sound silly," she said.

"No, not at all," Corbin admitted. "After our company started growing, Aiden and I had to get used to people thinking that they should have the freedom to look into our private lives. Hell, once Aiden started his run for your grandfather's vacant Senate seat, things got crazy. I can't leave work without being hounded by cameras and reporters screaming questions at me about my best friend."

"Yeah well, welcome to my everyday life," she sassed.

"I'm sorry," he offered. "Are you close with your parents?"

"No," Ava said without hesitation. "My mother died when I was just five and my father was left to raise me. Well, him and an army of nannies," she said.

"Army?" Corbin questioned.

"Yes," Ava said. "Unfortunately, my father used my nannies as his personal dating service. After my current nanny agreed to have sex with him, he moved her out and called the agency for another to be sent over. Honestly, I don't know how many he went through. I lost count after a while."

"Jesus, baby. I'm so sorry that you had to live that way," he said.

"It wasn't all bad. My dear father was too busy making his conquests to notice me and he occupied my nannies so I could do as I pleased, for the most part. If it wasn't for my grandfather, I would have been all alone in the world. My favorite memories were of the two of us just hanging out in his big old house when I spent the weekends with him." She shrugged, "At least I have Zara now, so I'm not completely alone."

Corbin hated the sadness that he saw in her eyes. He wished he could tell her that she wasn't alone, that he was there for her, but he also knew that things between them were still too new for such declarations.

"No brothers or sisters?" Corbin asked.

"I had a brother. He was older than me by ten years and we weren't close. He went away to college and that's when he disappeared. No one knows what happened to him," she whispered. Corbin remembered hearing something about the disappearance of the rich frat boy who was the Senator's son. He had no idea the kid was Avalon's brother.

"I remember that," Corbin said. "I was a teenager at the time it happened but I recall hearing the news stories about his disappearance. That must have been horrible for you."

"I know this makes me sound like a fucking awful

person, but like I said, we weren't very close. After my mother died, our family kind of fell apart. I had a very lonely childhood, except the time I had with Grandpa. I guess that's why I nabbed Zara up as soon as we met. She had no family and my own was broken. She used to come home with me on semester breaks from college. We'd celebrate Christmas with my Grandfather and she would tell me how lucky I was. I never had the nerve to tell her that my life wasn't as picture perfect as it seemed. I've never told anyone this—well, until now."

Corbin's heart beat a little faster and he wasn't sure how to respond to her admission. Hearing that she trusted him with her sad past made him want her even more—if that was possible. Still, a part of him wondered if it was futile for him to get his hopes up.

"Why tell me? Why now?" Corbin questioned.

"I'm not really sure," Ava admitted. "Talking to you is easier than I thought it would be. Maybe it's that I feel safe with you—I don't know," she said.

"Thank you, Ava." Corbin whispered. "I'm glad you feel safe with me. I'd never do anything to hurt you," he offered.

Well now, that remains to be seen, Corbin," she said. "Trusting you with my past is one thing, but I'm still not so sure I can trust you with my heart."

Corbin hated that she wouldn't trust him with everything but he understood that he had to earn that from her. "How about we just take this nice and slow?" he asked. "You know get to really know each other before we decide what we can and can't be."

"I think I'd like that," Avalon agreed. "How slow are we talking here?"

"Well," he thought. Corbin hated the idea of not ending up in bed with her again tonight. Every time he was near her, his body hummed to life and all he could think about was making her his again. But rushing Avalon into anything might be a giant mistake and one that could lose him his chance with her.

"How slow do you need me to go, Darlin'?" he asked.

AVALON

They had a quiet ride to the restaurant and all Ava could think about was Corbin's questions. Ava wasn't quite sure how to answer. She wanted to tell him to take her back to her room—or his for that matter and fuck her until she forgot everything but his name. Ava worried that might be more than he was planning for them tonight and she decided to just play things the way he wanted.

Plus, there was the whole subject she didn't share with Corbin when he was asking her questions about her past and her family. How did she just blurt out that she had to get married in the next month and a half or lose everything her beloved grandfather had left her? She had no problem telling Corbin what an ass her father was, but she conveniently left out the part where he conned her grandfather into putting a marriage clause in his will to try to trick her out of her money. Hell, the whole thing sounded crazy to her and maybe that was why she didn't share with Corbin. Ava hated

55

she was going to have to come clean with him but there was really no other way. Time was ticking and she had less than six weeks before her thirtieth birthday to find a man who wanted to marry her so she could claim her inheritance, keeping it out of her father's hands. It was the least she could do for her grandfather. She knew he wouldn't want any of his money going to his son. Ava remembered just how much her grandfather disliked her father and that made this whole thing so surreal. Why would her grandfather allow her dad to manipulate him into changing his will to add the marriage clause? It was something she planned on getting to the bottom to once she got back home. But for now, she had a very large, sexy problem that followed her to France and she needed to figure him out first.

They were seated in a private corner of the small Italian restaurant and Corbin seemed to have planned their evening down to the very expensive bottle of wine waiting for them on the small table. He helped her into her seat and sat so close to her, she was sure that they would elicit stares from other diners, but no one even glanced their direction.

The waiter poured them both a glass of wine, told them the specials and disappeared with a nod, promising to return soon to take their orders. Ava felt flustered and nervous suddenly being alone with Corbin again.

"You seem nervous again, honey," he chided, taking her hand in his own. Just that simple gesture had her relaxing some.

"I was just thinking about how I should answer your question," she admitted.

"My question?" he asked.

"Yes, the one about how slowly I'd like us to take this —well, whatever this is between us," she said.

"Don't think about your answer," he prompted. "Just tell me what you want, Ava," he said.

"How about we see how tonight goes and take our cue from there?" she questioned.

"I'd like that," he admitted. The waiter reappeared and Corbin asked if she'd mind if he ordered for the both of them. Honestly, she was happy to let him make that decision for her. Corbin threw her for a loop when he ordered in Italian and his shy smile after the waiter left just about made her swoon like a love struck teenage girl.

"I just realized that I know nothing about you, Corbin," she said. "You speak Italian?"

"Yes, Spanish, French and a little Russian too," he admitted.

"Wow," she breathed.

He shrugged, "It's not a big deal, really," he said, playing off his impressive talent.

"I'd like to know more about you," she said.

He held his arms wide, "I'm an open book, ask away," he offered, throwing her earlier words back at her.

"Tell me about your childhood," she asked.

Corbin chuckled, "Geeze honey, you should look into becoming a therapist," he teased. Ava knew he was avoiding her question but she was willing to wait him out. She sat back in her seat and smiled at him until

Corbin seemed to take the hint that she wasn't going to let him off the hook so easily.

"Well, you met my mother at Aiden and Zara's wedding," he started.

"Yes, Rose is lovely. She seems too young to be your mother though," she said.

Corbin's laughter filled the small room. "She loves to tell people I'm her brother. Honestly, she was way too young to have me. My mother got pregnant with me when she was just sixteen. It was a huge scandal in her little town and her parents all but disowned her for it. They tried to get her to abort the pregnancy but Mom refused and well, here I am," Corbin said motioning to himself.

"That's awful," Ava whispered.

"Yeah, my grandparents aren't the nicest people. They are still around but I don't see them much. My mother tries, she really does, but they treat her like crap still. All I have to say is my mother should be sainted for putting up with their bullshit." Corbin sipped his wine and when he didn't seem as if he was going to share anymore, Ava decided to pry a little deeper.

"And your dad?" she hesitantly asked. "Are you close with him?"

"No," Corbin said. "When my mom told him she was pregnant, he took off. He was quite a bit older and he didn't want to deal with the possibility of going to jail. When my grandparents threatened to press charges, he ran and the last my mother heard about him, he had ended up in prison for fraud and tax evasion."

"Wow," Ava breathed, "your poor mother."

Corbin shrugged, "She did just fine without the bastard, if you ask me. She raised me and let me tell you, that was no easy feat. When Aiden's mother took off and his father started drinking, mom took him in too."

"Have you known Aiden your whole life?" Ava asked.

"Since we were ten. He became my best friend and once my mother decided to basically take him in, he became like a brother to me," Corbin admitted.

"Kind of like Zara and me," Ava said.

"Exactly," Corbin confirmed.

"So, no brothers or sisters either?" she asked.

"Nope," he said. "Mom never really even dated when I was growing up. I guess she had her hands full with me and then Aiden."

"She had to have been lonely," Ava said. "How about now that you are both grown?"

"God no," Corbin growled. "The last think I want to even think about is my mother out with a man." Corbin made a face and she giggled.

"It wouldn't be as bad as that, Corbin. She's a beautiful woman and still young. Maybe she'll meet someone nice. Don't you want for your mom to be happy?" Ava asked.

"Not like that," Corbin admitted. "Mom has Aiden and she loves his girls as if they were her own grandchildren. I'd say her life is pretty full." Ava could tell that Corbin wasn't about to budge on the matter and she gave up trying to push the topic. Besides, it wasn't really her place to question whether or not Corbin's mother should or shouldn't be hitting the dating scene.

"So, you are pretty much up to speed on my childhood," he teased. Ava giggled. There was still so much she felt like she wanted to ask but Corbin seemed to be finished talking about himself.

"How long do you plan on staying in France?" Ava asked, changing the subject.

"That depends," he said.

"On?" she asked.

"On how long you will be in France. I came all this way, Ava and I don't plan on returning home without you," he admitted. Ava wanted to protest that Corbin couldn't just sit around and wait for her to finish her business all the while putting his life on hold, but judging from his determined look, he wasn't going to budge an inch on the subject.

"So that's your plan?" Ava asked. "You're just going to sit in your hotel room day in and day out waiting for me to finish up at work?"

"Naw, Darlin'," he said. "I have plenty of work to keep me busy and I was hoping to get you to agree to come back to my house and we could both get out of that cramped hotel," he said.

"Wait," Ava always felt as if she had to be on her toes around Corbin. He seemed to move at lightning speed and now was no exception. "You have a house here—in France?"

"Yep," he said. The waiter brought their food and Corbin waited for him to leave before filling her in on all the details. "It's not far from here. I'd love to take you by and give you a tour after dinner," he said.

Ava nodded, "I'd love to see your house," she admitted.

"Great," Corbin said. "Eat up and we can head out."

"You are full of surprises, Corbin," she admitted. Ava knew she was going to have to drop one major surprise of her own, but she also knew that timing was everything. She wanted one last night with Corbin and then she'd find a way to walk away. It was time for her to get her head on straight and either find a way around her father's latest scheme or come up with one damn good plan. One thing she knew for sure, she wouldn't drag Corbin into her family's drama or this mess with her father.

"Oh honey, I'm just getting started," he insisted. Ava wasn't sure if she should be excited or afraid of just how true he made that statement sound.

CORBIN

Corbin was having trouble reading Avalon. One minute she seemed to be on board with the possibilities of them testing the waters to see where this thing between the two of them was heading and other times she was cold and distant. It was almost as if she was trying to push him away.

He decided to show her his place just outside of town and hopefully convince her to spend the rest of her time with him while she was in France. If not, he'd be keeping his room right next to hers at the hotel. Either way, he didn't have any plans on letting sexy little Avalon out of his sight.

They finished dinner and he decided to let his driver go for the night. He drove the two of them out to his place and when they pulled in, he didn't miss the way Ava looked at his house. He took the fact that she was smiling as a good thing and when she got out of his car and practically ran up the steps to go into the front foyer, he knew she liked it.

"This is your place?" she questioned. "I pass this house on the way out of town, heading to the airport. I love this place. Doesn't it have a garden on the side with a little gazebo?" Corbin slyly nodded. He wasn't one to put much stock in where he lived. He still thought of the little shit hole that he and Aiden shared in college as his favorite home. But seeing the way his place brought out such excitement in Ava made him happy.

"How do you keep up with a place this big? You must come here a lot," she continued, spinning around the grand foyer as if checking over every square inch of the entryway.

"I have a housekeeper and a gardener who is also quite handy. Mr. and Mrs. Bisset are married and they take care of this place when I can't be here. I do like to spend most of my free time in France though," he admitted.

"Hmm," she hummed. "I never pegged you as a guy who'd vacation in France much less own a house here. I'm here a good bit of the year too—for work. It's almost crazy that we never ran into each other here since it's such a small town." Corbin had to admit he wondered the same thing.

He shrugged, "Well, you said you don't go out when you are here and I like to hit the clubs and do the whole French night life thing." Avalon wrinkled her nose, almost as if she smelled something bad.

"Yeah," she said. "I don't really care for the night clubs or bars in town. When I'm here, it's all business."

"We should do something about that," Corbin offered. "How about you let me take you out to some of the area clubs tomorrow night?" He didn't want to feel so nervous about asking her out again, but he was. Corbin felt as though he was holding his breath waiting for her answer.

"I don't know," she whispered. "I have a busy day tomorrow—lots of meetings."

Corbin nodded, not wanting to let her off so easily. He wanted more time with her and letting Ava come up with any excuse to avoid him, didn't play into his plans. "Then a quiet dinner in?" He asked, still hopeful.

"How about you give me a tour of your place and then we can talk about tomorrow," Ava offered.

"What's going on here, honey?" Corbin asked.

"I thought you were showing me your house," Ava said, resting her hands on her hips. It was her telltale sign that she was going to get shouty about something and it usually involved her stomping her little feet and making Corbin completely hot in the process.

"Sure, I'll show you around and then what?" Corbin asked. "I'm starting to get the feeling that you are going to give me the brush off and I have to tell you that won't work for me, Darlin'." Corbin pulled Ava against his body, but she refused to lower her arms that she had perched on her hips, making it damn near impossible to get close to her. The whole scene was almost comical but he knew better than to laugh judging from her very serious expression.

"I'm not sure what you want from me, Corbin," she sternly warned. "I thought we were just having fun and not making any promises."

"Fuck, Ava," he growled. "Are we seriously back to

the whole 'no promises' thing?" he asked. "I thought I was pretty clear when I explained that I want to make you some fucking promises," he shouted. Avalon pulled free from his hold and he instantly regretted his tone.

"You can't make me the kind of promises I need from you, Corbin. You're not ready for what I need right now and you might never be. I'm running out of time," she whispered.

Corbin wasn't sure why they suddenly had to worry about a time limit and he was pissed that Ava had already weighed and measured him. He wanted a fucking chance to prove himself, but she wasn't willing to even meet him halfway.

"I knew the score when I hopped into bed with you, Corbin. I told you it's fine. You like to play with subs at the club and I was one of them. You don't own me anything and I'm fine with that," she said.

"Well, I'm not fucking fine with any of it," he grumbled. "How many times do I have to tell you that I want more with you, Ava? You are the most stubborn woman on the planet."

"Gee, thanks for that," she teased.

"Really, Ava. How about you tell me what it is you don't think I'm willing to give you? What is it you need that I can't do or be for you?" he asked. Ava sat down on the small settee and looked up at him, almost as if pleading for him to take back his questions, but he wouldn't. It was time that they both laid their cards on the table and he was done with dancing around the truth.

"I want to get married," she whispered.

"And you don't think that I can give you that? I told you that I'm not playing at the club. Hell, I followed you all the way to France to tell you that I don't want anyone else but you. I was so afraid that you wouldn't make me any promises when you left because you wanted to date other men while you were here."

Ava barked out her laugh. "While I appreciate your grand gesture of showing up here to make sure I wasn't dating my way through the French male population, it's still not enough."

"Then tell me what else it is that I have to do to convince you that I'm ready to take a chance here, Ava," he said.

"Marry me," she offered.

Now it was Corbin's turn to laugh. "I'm flattered but don't you think we should go on a few more dates first?" he teased.

"How many more dates are we talking?" she asked.

Corbin crossed the room to sit down next to her on the small sofa. Red flags were waving like crazy and he knew that he was missing something but she wasn't giving any hints as to what it might be. He pulled Ava onto his lap and was surprised that she actually allowed him to hold her.

"Talk to me, Ava," he ordered. "Tell me what the hell is going on with you, please," he begged.

"I can't," she whispered. "You'll think I'm insane," she admitted.

"I already think that," he teased. "All I can piece together is that I'm crazy about you and I'd like to think you feel the same way about me," he said.

"I do," she whispered.

"Great, then why do you keep pushing me away and shooting me down at every turn? One minute, you seem to be happy and we're having fun and the next you can't even commit to another dinner."

"Tonight was going to be our last night together," she admitted. Before he could protest, Ava covered his mouth with her hand. "Please just let me finish," she demanded. Corbin nodded and sat back. He asked her to come clean with him and the least he could do was hear her out.

"Thank you," she said. "I need to get married and I know that isn't what you are looking for right now." Corbin opened his mouth to contradict her but quickly shut it again when she shot him a stern warning look.

"I know you say you want me and you'd like to see where this is going between us but I honestly don't have time to do that. About two weeks before you dared me to show up at the club, my father dropped a bomb that my inheritance, that I received from my grandfather, had a few strings and stipulations tied to the money."

"Marriage strings?" he asked.

"Yes," she said. "I have about six weeks to get married or my money goes to my father."

Corbin whistled, "Why would your grandfather do that to you?" he asked.

"I'm not really sure," she said. "My father said something about convincing him that by ensuring that I was married by thirty, it would also help make sure the family line continues. But, I don't buy that for a minute. I think my father had something he could use to blackmail my grandfather and that's how he got him to amend his will. Either way, I had my lawyers look at it and he's right. I now have just weeks before I either have to find a man and get married or lose everything."

Corbin wasn't sure if he wanted to ask his next question but he also had to know. "That night at the club—was that about this whole marriage deal?" God, that sounded worse out loud than it did in his head, if that was possible.

"No!" Ava shouted. "I'd never try to trap you or anyone else into marrying me, Corbin." She tugged his arms free and stood from his lap. "I'd rather lose my fortune than spend the rest of my life trapped in an unhappy marriage. Besides, you said it yourself—I've been pushing you away because I don't want to hurt you. That would be the last thing I want," she admitted.

Corbin felt like a complete louse for even asking his question. "I'm sorry but I had to know," he said. "But, what's the plan here, Ava? You push me away and then what? How were you planning on finding some guy to agree to marry you?"

"It's more complicated than that," she said. "Not only do I have to find some 'guy', as you put it, to marry me but we have to prove that we are committed and in love."

"What the fuck?" Corbin asked. "How will you prove that?"

"My father has hired a team of people to follow my new husband and I around to make sure we are truly as happy as we will hopefully portray. We would have to submit to questions and pass tests along the way. After our six- month anniversary, if my father can't prove that I've married for convenience and money, rather than love, I walk away with my money and he gets nothing."

"That sounds fucking awful," Corbin admitted. "How can your dad do that to you?" he asked.

"I told you we don't get along. My father has always been jealous of the relationship my grandfather and I had. I guess this is just his way of getting back at me," she admitted.

"Threats and interrogation seem like one hell of a way to go about getting back at someone, honey," he said.

"Yeah, but that's just a normal day for my family. It's one of the reasons why I try to steer clear of my father but now I don't really have a choice in the matter." Corbin could feel his wheels spinning and a plan forming. If he played his cards right, he'd be able to convince Avalon to give him a chance and be able to help her out with her situation.

"Okay," he agreed. Ava stopped pacing for a moment to look down to where he still sat.

"Sorry, okay what?" she questioned.

"Okay, I'll marry you," he said.

AVALON

Ava wasn't sure if she had heard Corbin correctly or if the exhaustion of traveling and work accompanied by the drama her father heaped on her, was all starting to catch up with her. She couldn't have heard him correctly, could she? Had Corbin Eklund just agreed to marry her?

"You can't be serious," she chided.

"Why the hell not?" he asked. Ava hated that she made him feel the need to defend himself but he couldn't mean what he said.

"Because you and I barely know each other. Did you not just hear a single word I said? I have to prove that my new husband and I are married for love and not convenience or money. You and I would have to submit to vigorous questioning and constantly being watched. We wouldn't ever be able to let our guards down for the next six months. I can't ask you to live like that, Corbin," she said.

"Fine, then don't ask. I'm offering, Avalon," he said.

"And what will you get out of the deal?" she questioned. Ava knew that Corbin was a shrewd businessman and he would want something in return.

"You." He shrugged. "I'd get you."

Ava giggled, "I think you're getting the raw end of the deal," she admitted.

"Not at all," he said. "Be my submissive," he offered. "You get a husband and I get a sub. We can get married and spend the next few weeks getting to know each other while we're in France. Then, by the time we go home, it won't be difficult to convince everyone that we are anything but a happily married couple, madly in love with each other."

"And at the end of six months, you'll be free to move on. You'll have to stick it out with me until the deadline," she said. Ava wanted to ask him for more but she really had no right to. He was offering her so much more than she ever hoped for and that would have to be enough for now.

"How about we just get through the next half of the year and then we can decide where we go from there?" he asked. Corbin held out his hand for her to shake, almost as if he were brokering a business deal.

"You'll be my submissive both in and out of the bedroom, Ava. In return, I'll be your husband and you get to keep your inheritance," he said.

Ava hesitated taking his hand. "You know first-hand that I'm a lousy sub," Ava said. "What happens if I disobey you?" She had a pretty good idea what his answer was going to be but she wanted to hear it for herself.

"I will come up with creative ways to punish that sexy ass of yours, honey," he admitted. "But, I will also reward you when you please me," he offered. The thought of having Corbin do anything to her made her skin feel warm and tingly all over. She couldn't seem to get the picture of him spanking her ass red out of her head and she started thinking of all the naughty things she could come up with to make that happen.

"I can see from the mischievous glint in your eye that I'm going to have my hands full with you, aren't I, Ava?" Corbin asked. She smiled and nodded.

"I won't lie," she said. "I like the idea of you spanking me when I misbehave," she sassed.

"I'll also withhold your release," he promised. "Only good girls get orgasms," he said. Ava pouted and he laughed. "Yeah, now you're getting it, honey."

"Do we have a deal?" he asked, still holding out his hand.

"Yes," she said, placing her hand into his and giving a firm shake. Corbin scooped her up into his arms causing her to squeal. "What are you doing?" she asked.

"I'm taking my new sub up to my bedroom and tying her to my bed," he said.

"But we need to talk about the wedding," she insisted.

"We can get married tomorrow as far as I'm concerned," he said. "Tonight, you are mine," he growled and Ava shivered from the promise she heard in his voice. She didn't want to admit that she would be his every night if he wanted her. She kept that bit of information to herself.

Corbin carried her up the stairs as if she weighed nothing and when he got to his master suite, he turned on the lights, causing Ava to blink against the brightness. "Are you going to leave those on?" she questioned.

"Yes," he said, pushing her up against the wall. Ava wrapped her legs around his waist and could feel his erection pushing into her core. Suddenly the idea of having the lights on seemed to frighten her a little less, especially with the way he was looking at her as if she was his next meal.

"Corbin, please," she whimpered, rubbing herself against him.

"Hold still, Ava," he demanded. "I'll take care of you but I won't allow you to top from the bottom."

Ava was still so new to this whole Dom/sub thing. She was sure that asking what topping from the bottom meant might get her into trouble but her curiosity got the better of her.

"Um," she squeaked as Corbin kissed his way down her jaw to her neck. "What exactly does that mean?" Ava wasn't sure if his heated gaze turned her on or scared the shit out of her.

"It means, Little One, that you are trying to take the upper hand. You are claiming to be submissive but trying to remain in control," he growled. She shot him a sheepish grin, not really trying to hide the fact that he was correct.

"Do you know what happens to pretty little subs who try to hold onto their control, Ava?"

She shook her head, "No," she admitted.

"No what?" Corbin demanded. Ava liked the way he

73

pushed her for more; it made her want to give him everything.

"No, Sir," she stuttered as he stared her down.

"Well, my beautiful submissive, why don't I just show you?" He lowered her to the floor and Ava reluctantly released her legs from his waist. Corbin pulled her along with him to his bed and he sat down on the end of the mattress. "Strip," he commanded.

"You want me to take my clothes off?" Avalon asked. She swallowed past the lump in her throat, not sure if she wanted to laugh or cry.

"Yes," he barked. "Slowly—take them off slowly. You remember your safe word?"

Ava remembered it and she worried that she was going to have to use it tonight, judging by the heat in Corbin's eyes, he wasn't going to go easy on her. "Yes," she said. "Ice cream."

"Good girl," he praised. "Now, strip," he said, reminding her of his original order. She had never taken her clothes off for a man while he watched before and she had to admit it made her downright uncomfortable. Ava tried to pull her zipper down but she was too nervous to get it to work.

"Turn around," Corbin ordered. She didn't hesitate, doing exactly as he asked. He slowly pulled the zipper down her back, letting his fingertips brush her skin as they went, eliciting shivers from her overly sensitive body.

As soon as he finished, he turned her back around so she was once again facing him. "Go on," he said. Ava smiled and let her cocktail dress slide down her body to reveal that she was wearing nothing underneath. She loved the way Corbin's breath hitched as he looked her bare body up and down.

"Fuck, if I had known you weren't wearing anything under that skimpy little dress all night, we wouldn't have made it through dinner," he admitted.

"So, you like? she questioned, spinning slowly around. Corbin gave a sharp slap to her ass and she yelped.

"Do you like, Sir?" he corrected.

"Sorry," she hissed. "Do you like, Sir?"

"Yes," he confirmed. "You are so fucking hot, Avalon. Now, it's time to get onto your punishment for topping from the bottom. You ready?" He looked at her as if he was staring her down waiting for her to safe word him already. Ava always loved a good challenge. If he was going to marry her, he would learn that fact soon enough.

"Yes Sir," she agreed. "I'm ready." Corbin chuckled and pulled her across his lap. Ava had tried spanking for pleasure during her training as a sub at the club back home. She had never been spanked as a punishment and she wondered if it would feel the same. She had to admit that she liked being spanked and she was hoping that Corbin wouldn't figure out that little fact until she was wet, completely turned on and getting off on his thigh.

"You will need to keep count," he ordered. "We are going to twenty and then we'll see how you feel from there."

"Yes Sir," she said. Corbin didn't give any warning,

just brought his palm down to land a firm slap on her right cheek. She yelped from the sting of his hand and choked out, "One."

He didn't bother with niceties like gently rubbing each blow to help her acclimate to his palm meeting her flesh. He wasn't sugar coating her punishment and God help her, Ava wanted to use her safe word but that would mean admitting defeat and that wasn't who she was. She kept count with him, blow for blow, just as he ordered.

"Eighteen," she finally cried out. Ava realized that her face was wet from her own tears and she wondered if Corbin would be able to tell that she had been crying. She hated the thought of giving him that satisfaction.

"Nineteen," she growled through her gritted teeth. The last blow was the hardest and nearly took her breath away, "Twenty," she sobbed. Corbin rubbed her ass and just the touch of his skin against her hot flesh was almost too much to bear. Ava was sure she wouldn't be able to sit down the next day and if she did, she would remember every single time Corbin's palm made contact with her ass.

Her heart was racing from the excitement of the whole scene and she wondered how she had gone her whole life without feeling this way with any other man. Her spanking made her feel things beyond just the physical pain and that scared the shit out of her. It was as if her world was spinning too quickly and all she wanted to do was make it stop so she could catch her breath for just a second.

Corbin helped her to stand and when he saw that

she had been crying, he stood and pulled her against his body. She didn't make a move to relax in his arms as he wrapped his own around her. "I didn't mean to make you cry, Ava," he said. "Tell me that you're alright," he demanded.

"You want me to lie then?" Ava choked. How could she tell him she was okay when she clearly wasn't? How did she explain to him that she wasn't hurt or upset about the punishment, but that it had quite the opposite effect, making her want things with Corbin and from him that she had never wanted with any other man?

"No, never," he said. He released her and she took a step away from him. The way he looked at her, as if she had hurt him, nearly did her in. "Ava," he said, reaching for her but she took yet another step back. She couldn't look at him anymore. It was all too much and she wasn't sure why she was having such a reaction to his punishment. "I just want to hold you, please," he begged.

Ava needed a minute to pull herself together and figure out what she wanted next. It was as if she couldn't think with him watching her the way he was, as if she was fragile and might break from what he had just done to her.

"I can't—I just need a few minutes," she begged.

"No, let me in, Ava," he said. "Just talk to me. Say something—anything."

"Ice cream," she said and turned to go into the adjoining master bathroom. Her mistake was looking back as she shut the door and seeing the hurt and confusion in Corbin's eyes. She just needed to get her shit together and hurting him wasn't part of the plan but it was too late for that. She had given him her safe word because she was a coward. He had made her feel too much, too fast and left her no other choice. Ava shut the bathroom door, effectively closing out the man who was beginning to own a piece of her heart and that was enough to make her want to scream her safe word from the rooftops.

CORBIN

A half hour had passed since Avalon used her safe word to hide from him in his bathroom. Corbin refused to leave his bedroom, taking up camp on his bed, waiting for her to come to her senses and come out of the bathroom. He could see all her raw emotions looking back at him through her tears and it gutted him. He knew that her spanking had release so much more than her disobedience. He could hear it in her voice every time she choked out her count and God help him; he could see it in her tear- stained cheeks when he finally released her body from his lap and she pushed him away. He felt the same hurt and panic he saw on her beautiful face and all he wanted to do was hold her and tell her that everything was going to be alright—but she wouldn't allow that. She said the only thing that would stop him from demanding that she obey him—her safe word.

He hated how she wasn't letting him in and talking about what had just happened between the two of them but he wouldn't force her to talk to him. Avalon's past with her father and lack of family support had to instill trust issues and he knew from his own experiences that breaking through those barriers would take time. Ava was worth the wait and effort he was going to have to give, but there would be no walking away from her—not now.

When she told him about the way her father had twisted and manipulated her grandfather to change his will, his heart ached for her. His father at least did him the favor of walking out on him and his mother before he could fuck them both up. Ava had to endure living with a dad who obviously didn't care what happened to her. He wanted to show her that not all men hurt women and that he especially would never do anything to hurt Ava. He wanted to be the person she turned to when things got rough and he was hopeful that someday she'd let him be that for her, but then she ran to hide in the bathroom, taking all his hope for their future together.

It was really a no-brainer when he had agreed to marry Ava. Hell, she was the first woman that he had ever entertained the possibility of marriage with. Avalon brought something out in him that he wasn't sure existed until they spent their one night together. He had no idea how they were going to make this whole thing work, but Corbin knew that he couldn't just let her walk out of his life and give some other asshole a chance to make her happy. Ava seemed determined to find a husband to beat her father's marriage clause and keep her inheritance. She seemed to be the type of woman who loved a good challenge and he knew from experience she wouldn't back down from her own father when he threw down the flag and challenged her to find a husband.

Ava cracked the bathroom door open and peeked out; not retreating into the dark bathroom after she found him sprawled across the bed. Corbin took that as a good sign and hoped that she was finally ready to talk. He just wanted a chance with her, but that wouldn't happen if Avalon continued to shut him out both metaphorically and physically.

"Hi," she whispered. He could tell by her tear-stained face that she had been crying in the bathroom and every one of his instincts were screaming at him to go to her and pull her into his arms but Corbin wanted Ava to come to him. She needed to meet him halfway if they were going to find a way to make this thing work.

"Hi," he said back, not moving from his spot on the bed.

"I—I'm sorry," she squeaked. "I freaked out and I ran. I'm sorry," she buried her face in her hands and sobbed. That was all he could take and Corbin was quickly by her side, pulling her into his chest to wrap his arms around her body.

"You have nothing to apologize for, honey," Corbin whispered into her hair. They stood there like that, Ava letting him hold her and he thought that might be the end of it. He wanted to talk about what had just happened between them but he didn't want to push.

"Want to talk about it?" He offered, trying to sound

casual about his offer. Ava wasn't the type of woman who liked to feel pressured into anything.

She shrugged and pulled free from his arms, grabbing the blanket that sat on the end of his bed, wrapping it around her bare body. "I told you that I had done some training as a sub?" she asked. Corbin nodded and sat on the chair across the room from where she stood. He knew she would need a little space and he was willing to give it to her, for now.

"Well, I did most of my training at the club but not all of it. Some I did here in France," she admitted. Corbin could tell by her expression that he might not like what she was about to say.

"Did someone hurt you?" he growled.

"No," she quickly admitted. "Not really. I like a little pain, or at least I thought I did."

"So, you're telling me you didn't like the spanking, but it wasn't for your pleasure," Corbin said. "Listen, if this is all too much for you—"

"It's not," she shouted. "Please, let me finish, Corbin." Ava was right to be mad at him, he was acting like an overbearing ass and that wasn't going to help things between them.

"Sorry," he grumbled. "You're right." He waved his hand at her to continue and she rolled her eyes at him.

"Thanks," she sassed. "I never really gave the whole BDSM thing a fair try. I would go into the club to work with a Dom here and there, but I never liked giving up that much control of myself. I had a few Doms tell me that I just wasn't submissive and that I should maybe look into becoming a Domme, but that never felt quite right either. I tried, really tried to do what they asked of me, but I didn't seem to get as much pleasure as they thought I should have from trying to meet their demands. I stopped training, believing that I just wasn't a submissive."

"Bullshit," Corbin interrupted and Ava shot him a look. He held up his hands in defense. "It's a fair statement, Ava. From everything you've shown me at the club and tonight, I would bet money you are submissive. Hell, I'd stake my life on it."

"That's the thing," she said. Ava paced the floor in front of him, letting the blanket fall around her shoulders and Corbin's palms itched to touch her bare skin again. "I thought I wasn't and I gave up entertaining the idea of ever having a Dom/sub relationship—until I met you. Our first night together opened up a whole new world for me and now, tonight I just can't explain it—I loved it."

Corbin let out his pent-up breath, not realizing he was even holding it. Hearing Ava admit that she liked what they had done so far made him want to demand more from her—he wanted everything, all of her, but he also needed to let Ava finish getting out whatever was bothering her. He didn't want to chance a repeat of her using her safe word to run to the bathroom to hide again.

"I wasn't sure what to expect from tonight. I've never been spanked as a punishment," she admitted. "I've been spanked for pleasure but tonight—what you did to me—it made me feel things I was never sure were possible."

"Like?" Corbin pushed. He was hoping they were at the same place, maybe even on the same page.

"Like, um—well, I might be falling for you," Ava admitted.

Corbin stood and closed the space between them, pulling her against his body again. "Yeah?" he questioned.

"Yes," she whispered. Corbin brazenly pushed the blanket from her body, leaving her completely naked.

"Well, you did agree to be my wife, so falling for me is a good thing, right?" Corbin asked.

"I said I might be falling for you and we both know you are marrying me just to help me out of a jam, Corbin," she said. Maybe it was time that he did some confessing, just as Ava was brave enough to do.

"What if I told you that I might be falling for you too and me asking you to be my wife was purely a selfish gesture?" Ava looked him up and down, as if she was trying to decide if she wanted to believe him or not.

"No," she breathed.

"Yep," he admitted. "So, no more hiding?" Corbin waited her out and when she nodded her agreement, he couldn't wait any more. He crushed his lips against hers, kissing and licking his way into her mouth. He loved her little breathy sighs and moans. Corbin was sure that he wasn't ever going to get enough of them or of Ava but he didn't give a fuck anymore. She was finally going to let him in and that was more than he could have ever asked for.

Ava was panting by the time he broke the kiss and smiled up at him. "I won't promise to be the perfect submissive. Hell, I'm probably going to fuck it up at every turn, but I want to try, Corbin," she said.

"Sir," he growled, giving her hair a light tug.

"Sir," she corrected.

"Maybe we should go over some ground rules and training, Ava," he said. She didn't exactly look thrilled about the prospect of him telling her what he expected from her and he almost wanted to laugh as she groaned and nodded her agreement.

"Fine," she agreed. "Just as long as you promise that we are going to get to the part where you take your clothes off and we get to actually have sex." Corbin swatted her ass, causing her to yelp. He knew she had to still be sore from her spanking. He didn't go easy on her and he wouldn't ever promise to. It was just who he was and the sooner Ava learned that, the better.

"First step of your training is going to be learning not to top from the bottom, Baby Girl," he said.

"I told you that I suck at being a submissive," she said, rubbing her ass with her hands.

He grinned, knowing she didn't pick up on her pun but it wasn't a bad idea. "Let's see just how well you can suck as my submissive," he said. Corbin pushed her body down until Ava took the hint and sunk to her knees before him. He unzipped his pants, letting his cock spring free and Avalon hissed out her breath.

"Finally," she almost cheered.

"That remark just earned you another punishment," he said.

Ava covered her ass with her hands, "Please no," she begged. "My ass is already raw."

"I know, honey," Corbin soothed, running his hand down her soft face. "But, I have other lovely ways of punishing you without hurting that sweet ass of yours any further." He thought of all the wicked ways he could teach Ava obedience and he had to admit that he hoped she was as mouthy and spunky as he knew she could be. It would give him plenty of opportunity to do ever naughty thing he was thinking and then some.

"I don't think I like the sound of that and I definitely don't like that look on your face," she whined. Corbin chuckled. His Ava was definitely submissive but she was the most reluctant sub he had ever had. Corbin wasn't sure how he was going to tame her and maybe he'd never be able to, but he was going to have a fucking fantastic time trying.

"Oh honey, I'm just getting started," he admitted. "Now open that sweet, sassy mouth of yours," he ordered.

AVALON

Ava wasn't sure if she felt giddy or scared kneeling in front of Corbin as he stroked his heavy shaft waiting for her to comply. She wanted everything he was offering her; that wasn't a question. Ava worried that if she fell completely for Corbin Eklund, her heart wouldn't survive.

He stroked a hand down her face, forcing her to look up at him. "You don't have to do anything you don't want to, honey." She knew that as a submissive, she had the power to make her own decisions. Ava just worried that she was making the right one. She smiled up at him and opened her mouth.

"I want this," she said. She reached for his cock, wrapping her hands around his shaft and helped to place the head into her open mouth.

"Thank fuck," Corbin exclaimed and thrust himself a little further in. He caressed her face again and her heart was nearly undone by his gentleness. "That's so good, baby," he praised. "Yes, just like that," he moaned as she sucked him to the back of her throat and swallowed around him. Corbin stroked in and out of her willing mouth a few more times and then pulled free. Ava didn't hide her frustrated groan and he chuckled.

"I know, honey," he soothed. "But I want to be inside of you when I come," he said. Corbin helped Avalon from her kneeling position and ordered her up onto his bed.

"I'm going to handcuff you to my bed and then I'm going to fuck you until neither of us has any strength left." Ava whimpered at his promise, not sure she was still capable of making coherent words. She watched as Corbin secured first her wrists and then her ankles to his bed posts using handcuffs. She was completely sprawled out and vulnerable to whatever he wanted to do with her.

Corbin stood back from the bed and looked her over, as if admiring his own handy work. "Fuck, baby," he growled. "You look good enough to eat." Ava smiled up at him and he shook his head. "Later, baby. Right now, I need to fuck you," he admitted.

Ava felt the bed dip with his weight and Corbin ran two big fingers through her drenched pussy, checking to see if she was ready for him. She knew that he'd find her more than ready to take him. She tried to rub herself against his fingers, needing more, bucking against her restraints.

"Hold still, Ava," he ordered. "You will hurt yourself if you keep thrashing about." He was right; the bite of the metal handcuffs was more than uncomfortable.

"Please, Corbin," she moaned.

"Sir," he reminded.

"Please, Sir," Ava corrected. "I need you."

"It's okay, baby. I'm going to take good care of you," he promised. He knelt between Ava's legs and thrust balls deep into her body, not giving any warning. Corbin pumped in and out of her drenched pussy, using her body and giving her so much pleasure in return. Ava began to lose track of her orgasms and she didn't remember him unlocking her cuffs and pulling her onto his lap to straddle his cock. He ruthlessly pumped in and out of her body and just when she thought she wouldn't be able to take anymore, he snaked his hand down between their bodies and stroked her sensitive clit, sending her soaring.

"That's right, baby," he crooned. "Come with me," he said. He pumped into her body a few more times and shouted her name when he came.

"Thank you," she whispered, lying limp in his arms.

"Never thank me for that," he said. "It's my pleasure." Corbin rolled them to the mattress and pulled her against his body, wrapping her in his arms. Ava was sure she had never felt more secure or protected in her life and dare she ever dream it possible—loved.

The next morning Avalon woke and found the bed empty, but the smell of bacon and coffee wafting down the hall from Corbin's kitchen was enough to wake her up. She found his shirt from the night before lying on the chair in the corner of the room and she pulled it onto her bare body.

Ava wasn't quite sure where his kitchen was, not really having a full tour of his house the night before, but she followed the smell and the racket Corbin was making. She found him standing at his stove, flipping pancakes in just his boxers and Ava suddenly forgot that she was hungry or in dire need of coffee.

"Morning," she said, seeming to startle him. His big body jumped and she love the way his muscles bunched and flexed, really giving her a good view of his tattoos. He was even more gorgeous in the morning light, if that was possible.

"Hey," he said. "Sleep well, beautiful?" Corbin turned off the stove and poured her a cup of coffee, handing it to her and then carefully pulled her into his arms for a kiss.

"I did," she admitted. "Best sleep I've had in a long time. In fact, I woke up wondering just where I was and that hasn't happened for quite some time."

"Well, I hope you don't make a rule of waking up at strange men's homes in France and forgetting where you are," he teased. She swatted at him and when he let her go, she sat down at his kitchen table and gulped down half her coffee.

"You're up early," she said.

"Yeah, jet lag," he admitted. "I don't sleep well when I'm not at home," he said.

"You should have woken me up," Ava offered. "I'm sure we could have found something to do together to make you tired again," she said and giggled.

"Hmm," he hummed. "You might just be a decent submissive after all," he joked.

"Speaking of being submissive," she said. "Don't we have some rules to go over or something?" She hated the idea of putting rules in place to govern what she hoped was a relationship between the two of them, but Corbin was right last night when he said she could use some more training.

"How about we discuss those tonight?" Corbin offered. "I don't want you to be late for work and I can pick you up and we can have a quiet dinner here, if you'd like." Ava's heart seemed to beat a little faster when she heard him mention them going back to his place again. Honestly, she loved his house and staying there was so much nicer than her hotel, but she didn't want to read into the situation or get her hopes up, only to have them dashed.

Corbin chuckled, "you are way over thinking all of this, Darlin'. I'd like to have dinner with you tonight and if you're okay with the idea, I'd like for you to move out of your hotel and in here with me," he offered.

Ava didn't take any time to think his offer over. Honestly, she didn't need to. After last night, she was willing to do just about anything the gorgeous man sitting next to her wanted, although she'd never admit that to him.

"I'd like that," she said. "I can have the hotel send my things over and that way I won't have to waste time packing later." Ava didn't miss the guilty grimace on Corbin's face and she sighed, "I'm not going to like what you are about to tell me, so just spill it," she ordered.

"I kind of already had the hotel send your belongings over and they are in the foyer." Corbin held up his hands as if in defense and gave her his sexy smirk. "Before you get angry with me, I did it so you'd be able to get dressed this morning; not because I assumed you'd say yes to my offer."

"But you had a hunch?" She questioned.

"Well, not so much a hunch as I was hopeful," he admitted.

"Fine," she said around a mouthful of pancake. "But, we are definitely going over some ground rules tonight —for both of us." She pointed her finger at him, for good measure and Corbin smiled and nodded.

"Deal," he agreed. "Finish eating your breakfast and I'll run you a bubble bath. We have just enough time for one, if you hurry," he said. Ava shoved a few bites of bacon into her mouth and Corbin laughed again.

"What?" she asked. "I love a good bubble bath. I'm assuming you will be joining me?"

"Only if you behave yourself," he teased. "I have a meeting this morning and I can't be distracted by your feminine charms."

Ava smiled up at him, "A girl can try," she said, watching as Corbin stacked some dishes in the sink and then disappeared down the hall to his master bedroom.

"A girl can try," she whispered again to herself.

Avalon felt as if her meetings would never end. Her day

seemed to drag on with no end in sight and she had a feeling that had everything to do with the sexy man who texted her every hour to tell her how much he missed her. Honestly, she felt the same way and was counting down the minutes until he was supposed to pick her up.

Ava told Corbin that she'd find her own way home, but he insisted that he had business in town and would be around at six to pick her up and he was. She walked out of her office building to find her sexy as sin Dom standing by the back door of his SUV, arms crossed over his massive chest, waiting for her. She couldn't read his expression behind his dark sunglasses, but judging by the sexy smirk on his face, he was happy to see her.

"You brought your driver?" she asked, hating that he went to any fuss over her. "I could have called for a car and met you back at your place."

Corbin sighed and opened the back door. "I brought my driver so that you and I can talk about our days and God, I've wanted to do this since dropping you off this morning—" Corbin pulled her into his arms and sealed his mouth over hers, kissing her as if he hadn't seen her in months and not just hours. She felt as if he was touching every inch of her body, being pressed up against his and she could think of nothing she wanted more than for Corbin to take her home and strip her bare.

"There," he panted. "That's so much better." He let Ava slide down his body and when she felt his erection jutting into her belly she gasped. Corbin's wolfish grin told her everything she needed to know—he had the same plans as she had for their evening together.

"Wow," she stuttered. "You really missed me," she teased. Ava daringly snaked a hand down between their bodies and cupped his erection through his pants, loving the way his breath hissed out and he leaned into her touch.

"That feels so fucking good, baby," he said. "But this isn't the time or place." He pulled her hand into his own and kissed her fingers, as if trying to ease his rejection. She knew she was pouting but she didn't care. There was just something about Corbin Eklund that made her feel daring and want to take risks.

"I promise honey, as soon as we get into my car, you can have free reign," he said. Ava wasted no time, pushing past him to eagerly climb into the back of his SUV. Corbin chuckled and slid into the back seat next to her. "You seem pretty determined to have your way with me, Darlin'," he drawled.

"Well, I'm sure you offering free reign over your body isn't going to happen very often. I want to take advantage of your generosity while it lasts," she said. Corbin threw back his head and laughed and Ava was sure she had never seen a more beautiful man in her life.

Corbin raised the privacy partition, separating them from his driver and pulled her onto his lap. Avalon straddled his thighs and framed his face with her hands.

"Hi," he whispered, palming her ass through her clothing.

"Hey," she said. "I missed you today," she admitted. Ava almost felt silly saying those words out loud. Really they hadn't been in each other's lives for very long and the time they did spend together was because their two best friends sort of threw them at each other. But now, since their one night together at the club, she was beginning to see another side to Corbin and she had to admit, she liked it. Sure, she loved his dominance—craved it even but there was more to him than that.

He pulled her down and sealed his lips over hers, licking his way into her mouth. He broke their kiss long enough to whisper that he missed her too and Ava was sure that she had just lost another piece of her heart to him. She needed to be careful with those pieces because if she didn't keep them safely guarded, Corbin Eklund would end up with her whole heart and she wasn't sure how she felt about that.

CORBIN

Corbin wanted to get Ava naked and beneath him more than he wanted his next breath but they needed to go over a few things first—namely rules to govern their relationship. She wasn't going to like all of them, but they were necessary to protect them both and he hoped Ava knew enough about Dom/sub relationships to understand their necessity.

When Ava seemed determined to get them both naked again, as fast as humanly possible, he tugged on her hair and she sat back, seeming to take his subtle hint that she was topping from the bottom again. He liked that she was a quick study, but he was pretty sure that his new little sub was going to give him more trouble sooner or later and she'd be right back over his knee taking her punishment.

"Rules," he breathed.

"What about them?" Ava sassed. He swatted her ass and she yelped.

"We need to go over them to make sure you are

comfortable with what's about to happen between us," he said.

"I'm pretty sure that what is about to happen between the two of us is already happening, Corbin," she teased. Ava ran her hand over his erection which was still trapped in his pants and he groaned. All he wanted to do was let her have her way but he knew that would get them no closer to having rules in place. He was a Dom down to his core and he needed order and rules to make sense of any of what was going on between them. This was all so new for him; Corbin needed some familiarity to get himself feeling back on track again, but he was pretty sure that being tangled up with sexy Ava would never afford him such comforts.

"You keep giving me reasons to want to punish you, baby," he warned. Corbin didn't miss the way Ava's eyes seemed to flare with need every time he mentioned punishment. He knew his little vixen liked it a little rough in the bedroom.

"What kind of punishment are we talking, Corbin?" she playfully asked.

He swatted her ass again but this time instead of her surprised yelp, he was gifted a sultry moan as her reaction. "You are trying to get me to spank your ass, aren't you, baby?" He asked. She slyly nodded and smiled, rubbing her hot core all over his lap. Even through all their clothing, he could feel her wet heat.

"You don't have to misbehave for me to spank you, Darlin,'" he promised. "I'll gladly spank your ass red if that's what you'd like for me to do. All you have to do is ask."

"Please," she begged. "Please spank me, Sir," she said. He loved the way he didn't have to remind her to call him that when they were roleplaying or having sex. She seemed to slip into her part with ease in just the short time that they had been together.

"Good girl," he praised. Ava all but purred and rubbed herself against him, seeming to need the contact. "Lie over my lap and pull your skirt up over your hips, honey," Corbin ordered. "I think we have time for a spanking and a few rules, if we multitask. You up for a game?" He asked. Ava nodded and inched her black skirt up over her hips, just as he asked, gifting him with the view of her bare pussy. He loved that she went sans panties all day. He liked to think that she spent her day wet and thinking about him every time she shifted in her seat, especially after the spanking he gave her the night before.

"Yes, Sir," she agreed. Ava lay across his lap with her curvy little ass up and he moaned and caressed each cheek, giving them each a light smack.

"I'm going to give you a rule and if you agree to it, you get a smack. If you don't, then nothing." Corbin knew his game wasn't fair and when Ava practically tried to sit up on his lap to protest, he wanted to laugh. She really was going to give him trouble at every turn. Corbin pushed her back down and ordered her to obey or use her safe word. Although, after what happened the night before, he hoped like hell she wouldn't ever have to use her safety net again.

"That's not fair, Corbin," she complained. "You can't

force me to agree to your rules by offering to give me what I want."

"Sir," he growled.

"Okay—that's not fair, Sir," she corrected. He smacked her ass and she moaned and rubbed her wet folds against his thigh.

"Hey, you tricked me," she said. "This game is rigged," she accused. Corbin planned on using every trick he could to get her to comply.

"Maybe so, Darlin'," he agreed. "But I'm going to teach you that I always get my way and after you learn that little lesson, I'm going to fuck you until I'm sure the driver can hear you screaming my name." He picked up his cell phone and ordered his chauffer to drive for another hour—he didn't care where. When he ended his call, he looked down to find Avalon looking up at him and he knew she wasn't going to easily agree to any of this, but that was something he could fix. Corbin always liked a challenge and Ava sure did give him one.

"First rule," he said. "When we are together, in this way—" He palmed her bare backside and she thrust her ass into his hands. "You will obey me and call me Sir." Corbin took a breath before saying the next part. This was where his little Avalon might give him some trouble.

"Agree or disagree?" he asked.

She smiled up at him and for a split second, he worried that she was going to disagree. "Agree," she said. Corbin wasted no time landing the first blow on her ass and she moaned and thrust back against his palm, anticipating the sharp smack.

Rule number two," he continued. "You will wear what I pick out for you when it's just the two of us—you know, like around the house and when we go to dinner."

Ava started to sit up again and Corbin pushed her back down onto his lap. "Corbin," she protested.

"Rule number one," he shouted.

"Fine—Sir," she said. "You can't dictate what I wear out in public, when we go to dinner. I'm part owner of a fashion company and I can't wear a competitor's brand. I agree to wear whatever you like when we are in the privacy of your home," she said.

Corbin thought about her offer. He knew her job was important to her and she was right, wearing a competitor's clothing brand wouldn't be good for her business. He could also show Avalon that he wasn't being an asshole just for the sake of it.

"Alright," he agreed. "We can take me dressing you to go out in public off the table as long as you're willing to add that when we go to a club, I get to pick your outfit."

"Club?" Ava questioned. "Like a night club?"

"No," he said. "Like the BDSM club, when we go to play."

Ava smiled up at him and nodded. "I agree," she said. Corbin raised his hand and let his palm fall to meet her ass with a hard slap. Ava moaned and wiggled on his lap as he caressed her skin where he landed the blow.

"You do like this, don't you baby?" he asked.

"Yes," she admitted.

"I can feel how wet you are and you smell so fucking good," he whispered, dipping two fingers into Ava's wet folds and running them through her pussy. He liked the way she writhed against his fingers, seeming to need more. "Not quite yet, baby," he teased. Ava mewled her protest, causing him to chuckle.

"Rule three," he said, running the pad of his thumb over her sensitive clit, giving her just a taste of what her impending orgasm was going to feel like once he let her get off. "I want to take you to a club to play at least a few times a month, if not more. Even after we're married, I'd like to continue to play with you at the club," he said.

Ava didn't even look up at him this time. She simply nodded, "Agreed," she said. Corbin landed another blow to her ass liking the way it was starting to turn a pinkish shade.

"Rule Four," he continued. "I control all of your orgasms. You will not touch yourself unless I tell you to and you don't come until I allow it," he said.

"Fine," she said. "I don't really like to do that anyway," Ava admitted.

Corbin stilled, "You don't like to touch yourself?" he asked. Ava looked back at him and shook her head, scrunching up her nose at the thought of it. Honestly, he had the exact opposite reaction when he thought of her touching her wet pussy to get herself off.

"Fuck, honey." He smacked her ass and ordered her to sit up on his lap. She did as he asked and he spread her legs wide over his own. "I need to see you touch yourself now," he ordered.

"But you just said—" she started to protest. Corbin pinched her taut nipple between his fingers and she yelped.

"I don't need to be reminded of what I just said, Avalon. I told you that you wouldn't touch yourself until I ordered it. I'm telling you to slide those sexy fingers down your thighs and run them over your wet pussy, nice and slow so I can watch," he ordered.

Ava hesitated and he wasn't sure if she was going to follow his orders, but when she finally slid her hands down her thighs, he thought for sure he was going to come in his own fucking pants—she was so hot. He looked down her body as he held her to his own and watched as her fingers easily glided through her slick folds and when she pulled them free, all he could think about was tasting her.

"Show me, Ava," he growled. She held her wet fingers up, as if allowing him to inspect them and he pulled them to his mouth and sucked them in, humming his approval around her fingers.

"That's so fucking hot," she whispered.

"Yes, it was," he agreed, guiding her hand back down her body. "Do it again but this time, don't stop until I tell you to." He knew he was going to test her but it was time to see what his girl was made of. "And Ava—don't come," he added. She groaned and slid her fingers through her pussy and it was all he could do to concentrate on what rule number he was on.

"Rule five," he whispered into her ear. Corbin couldn't keep his hands to himself, running them up and down her sensitive nipples. She bucked on his lap and he grabbed her thighs, spreading them further apart and holding them down on his own. He kissed a path up and down her neck and gently bit into her shoulder, causing her to cry out his name. He knew she was close but he didn't want to let her come yet.

"Five," she almost shouted, she was so on edge.

"This thing between us is exclusive. You won't be with anyone else unless I feel we need to bring a third in for our roleplaying at the club," he said. Although the thought of someone else touching Ava both turned him on and pissed him off all at the same time. He'd have to figure all that out later—for now, she was his and only his.

"Agreed," she moaned. "But you too," she amended. "No one but me," she panted. That was an agreement he could honor.

"Yes," he said. "You are so fucking beautiful right now," he praised. Corbin watched as Ava worked her fingers in and out of her pussy, trying to stay off her impending orgasm.

"Please," she whimpered. He wanted to give her what she needed. Hell, he wanted to give her the whole fucking world, if she'd let him.

"Come for me, my beautiful girl," he ordered and that seemed to be all she was waiting for. Ava had obeyed his every command and agreed to most of what he wanted. She was his; body, mind and soul and Corbin wasn't sure which he wanted to command first. All he knew was his once reluctant submissive was finally becoming everything he ever could have dreamed of in a partner and Corbin knew he was holding his entire world in his arms.

AVALON

Ava felt as if her body was floating on a cloud and hearing the sweet praises from Corbin made her heart feel as though it was soaring along with her. As far as rules went, Corbin's demands weren't completely unreasonable and she had to admit, she was happy they were in place. They both knew exactly where the other stood except she wasn't ready to admit that she was falling in love with him. Her feelings had nothing to do with his rules and their relationship and it was time she remembered that and kept them separate.

"That was—" Ava wasn't sure how to finish her sentence. Saying that it was wonderful wasn't quite right. Hell, it was everything but that sounded down-right sappy.

"Yeah," Corbin agreed. "I need you," he said. Ava realized that she had been completely greedy and forgot to take care of him and judging from the erection practically bulging out of his pants, Corbin looked about ready to explode.

"Yes," she agreed. "You do need me." Ava ran her hands over his cock and he hissed out his breath.

"Clothes off," he ordered. Ava hesitantly looked out the window and he growled. "No one can see us, Ava. The windows are heavily tinted and your hesitation might just earn you a punishment."

"What kind of punishment, exactly?" Ava asked. She watched as Corbin unzipped his pants, letting his cock spring free. He let his hands glide over his shaft and Ava licked her lips, wanting nothing more than to taste him.

"No, baby. If I let you get your sexy lips on my cock, I'll be coming down your throat in seconds. Besides, I promised that you can ride my cock until I have you screaming out my name," he reminded. Avalon smiled and nodded. She quickly tugged her shirt up over her head and Corbin helped her out of her skirt. He looked her over like a wolf would look at its prey and Ava shivered. He was always so intense, from the way he watched her to the way he made love to her and she was sure she'd never get tired of his demands.

"Straddle me," he ordered. She did as he asked and Corbin held her hips, lowering her onto his cock until she was fully seated. He pulled her down and sealed his mouth over hers, pumping into her, taking what he needed.

"You feel so fucking good," he moaned against her neck. "Move for me, Ava," he demanded. Ava threw her head back and rode his cock, taking every ounce of pleasure he was offering her. "Yes," he groaned. "Don't stop, I'm going to come." Corbin pumped into her a few more times and just when she thought she couldn't take anymore pleasure from him, another orgasm slammed through her core and she shouted out his name. Corbin followed her over and pulled her down on top of his body.

"See," he said. "I told you I'd have you screaming out my name before we got back home." Ava giggled against his chest and he tightened his arms around her body.

"I think I could get used to this," Ava whispered.

"Me too, honey," he admitted.

"Tomorrow's Saturday," Corbin reminded. "Do you have to go into work?"

Ava knew that she really should go in for at least a few hours but the thought of having to spend the day away from Corbin again felt pointless. She would just spend the time in her office wondering what he was doing and if he missed her, as she had today.

"No," she lied. "I have the whole day free."

Corbin's smile nearly made her heart stutter. "Good," he said. "I thought we could get married," he said.

"Married?" Ava asked. He offered to marry her when she told him about her dilemma with her grandfather's will, but a part of her didn't believe that he would follow through. She should have known that when Corbin Eklund made an offer, he lived up to his promise.

"You'll really marry me tomorrow?" She asked. She had been marking off the days until her time was up— her thirtieth birthday was only weeks away and it felt as if she was going to lose everything just because of a stupid stipulation. Ava hated that her father might win and take away everything her grandfather worked so hard for.

"Honey, I'd marry you any day of the week. I meant it when I said that I want to help you out. Your father won't even know what hit him," Corbin said. Ava didn't want to admit she was hurt by the fact that he wanted to marry her to help her win a legal battle. She was a fool to believe this thing between them was anything more to him.

Ava sat up and found her clothes, pulling them back on and sliding into her seat. "Yes, thank you," she said. Her voice sounded a little colder than she planned but she didn't care. "I'd be happy to marry you tomorrow."

"I've scheduled an appointment for two o'clock," he said. Ava looked out the window at the passing landscape, refusing to look at Corbin. She wouldn't let him see her hurt or disappointment.

"Ava," Corbin said. "Please look at me," he asked.

When she shook her head and wiped at the hot tears that now spilled down her face, his frustrated growl filled the cabin of his SUV. "Fuck, Ava," he shouted. "Stop hiding from me and tell me what's going on," he ordered.

Ava chanced a look at him and the anger and concern she saw on his handsome face nearly took her breath away. "Is this what you want to see?" she spat. "Me crying over something that will never be? Me getting upset about something you never offered me but my stupid mind believed to be a possibility?"

"I don't think I'm following, honey," he said. "I told

107

you that I'll marry you. I thought that was what you wanted."

"It is," she groaned. "But I thought that when I got married, it would be to a man who wanted to be with me. Not to someone who was doing me a favor to keep my money. You said it yourself, Corbin; you're doing this to help me out."

"No," he breathed. "I'm doing this because you are all I can fucking think about anymore, Ava. Ever since I met you, I've been looking for a way into your life—a way to get you to agree to even give me a chance and now that you have, there is no fucking way I'm letting you walk away from me. I want to marry you because I want you—all of you. I think I'm falling in love with you, Avalon," he admitted.

Ava's breath hitched and she wasn't sure what she should do next. She felt like cheering and fist pumping the air but she was sure that wasn't the right reaction.

"Tell me you feel the same way," Corbin ordered. "Fuck, just say something."

Ava climbed back onto Corbin's lap and snuggled against his body. "I'm falling in love with you too," she admitted. "And, I will gladly marry you tomorrow or any other day of the week," she said, giving him back his own words. "I can't wait to be your wife."

Corbin had thought about everything, right down to having her partner meet her at his house to help her throw together a dress for their special day. They practically made a wedding dress from scratch, staying up half the night to do it but Ava wouldn't have changed a thing. When she found Corbin standing at the bottom of the steps waiting for her in his black suit, she couldn't help but feel like the luckiest woman on the planet.

"Wow," he said as she walked down the long staircase in the dress she helped to design. The front was cut just below the knees but the back had a train that trailed behind her on the floor, covered in sequence and beads that she had hand sewn onto the dress.

"You look fantastic," he said, taking her hand to help her down the last few steps.

"Thanks and you look pretty fantastic yourself," she said back. "Are you sure you want to do this today?" Ava had heard Corbin on the phone with his mother, Rose, who was back in the States. He was trying to find a way around the major snowstorm that had grounded his private jet and every other plane on the East Coast, effectively trapping his mother and Aiden from making the trip over to France for their ceremony. Ava was sad that Zara was too pregnant to travel, but there was no way she'd chance her best friend's health or that of her god child. She told Zara that she and Corbin would plan a special ceremony for friends and family when they got back to the States. Ava kept the fact that the clock was ticking and they were racing time to get hitched to herself. Her best friend might not be too happy to hear that Corbin was marrying her to help her keep her inheritance. Zara wouldn't understand. Hell, Ava didn't really understand this whole mess but she wasn't going to overthink it too much. She wanted Corbin, anyway she could get him and if that meant marrying him without any promise in place for their future together then so be it. Sure, he had admitted that he was falling for her but that really didn't mean anything. He didn't come out and say that he was in love with her and maybe he wasn't. And, for now, that was okay with her.

She could see the sadness in Corbin's eyes at the reminder of his mom and best friend not being able to make it. "It's like you told Z, we can just have another ceremony for our friends and family when we get home. Mom is already planning it and hopes that you'll let her help."

"Of course," Ava agreed. "I love Rose." She meant it too. Corbin's mom was one of the nicest people she had ever met. She loved the way Rose took care of Zara when she and Aiden were just starting out. She'd always be grateful to Rose for the way she helped her best friend.

"Then today can be just for us," Corbin whispered. She nodded and Corbin wrapped his arms around her body. He smelled as good as he looked and from the way he was watching her, he was ready to get to the honeymoon portion of their evening. "Good, I've made us an appointment at the courthouse. We will be married in an hour—any regrets?" He seemed to be waiting her out as if she would protest marrying the sexiest man she'd ever met. Sure, she wished the circumstances were different, but he did admit that he was falling for her and if she wasn't such a coward, she'd fully admit that she was already in love with him.

But she was too afraid to let herself hope that what had started as a scheme for her to keep her money could possibly lead to her finding her happily ever after.

The drive to the courthouse took less than five minutes, but it was long enough to give her time to rethink everything that had happened over the past couple weeks.

"Nervous?" Corbin questioned. She shook her head and he laughed. "Liar," he accused. "You look like you are about to open that fucking door and run from this car as fast as those sexy heels will carry you."

"Well, the thought has crossed my mind," she admitted.

"Don't," he barked. "I'm not sure what is going through that pretty little head of yours but just cut it the fuck out," he ordered. "I want to do this, Avalon. I wouldn't have offered otherwise. You need to stop over-thinking all of this and just let it happen."

"But—" she tried to protest but Corbin wasn't having it. He sealed his mouth over hers and by the time he let her up for air, she completely forgot what she was going to say.

"But nothing," he said. "Ready?" Corbin asked, reaching out his hand for hers. This time, Ava didn't hesitate. She took his hand and allowed him to help her from his SUV and she didn't let go until the judge pronounced them husband and wife and told Corbin to kiss his bride.

He pulled her against his body and kissed her as if they weren't standing in the middle of a courthouse surrounded by about fifty strangers. It wasn't what Ava had dreamed about when she thought of her wedding day. In fact, it was probably the exact opposite of what she planned but it was perfect. She even got a little choked up when the judge asked her to recite her vows after him. They were lucky that he spoke English because her French was a little rusty. Of course, Corbin spoke perfect French and even said his vows in it. She barely understood him, but when he got to the part where he had to say, "I do", he said it in English, gifting her with a sexy wink. She giggled at his theatrics and judging by the swoon of the women in the crowd, they were buying into his performance too.

And when he was finally allowed to kiss her, she could feel her own heart beating wildly in her chest and Ava knew right then and there that she was a goner. Her heart was his whether he knew it or not and when or even if this thing between them ended, she would never find another man that made her feel the way Corbin Eklund did.

"Well Mrs. Eklund," he whispered into her ear. "You ready to get the honeymoon portion of this marriage thing started?" Corbin asked.

"Yep," she agreed. "As long as I report back to work Monday morning, I'm all yours until then." He smiled a wolfish grin down at her and she didn't hide the shiver that ran up the length of her spine. He knew exactly the effect he had on her and she was pretty sure that he was going to live up to every silent promise he was making her.

"That works," he agreed. "I have a little wedding present I'm hoping you like," he said. Corbin beat a path out of the courthouse like a man on a mission and pulled her along behind. Ava could barely keep up between tripping over her dress and falling over her heels.

"Corbin," she complained. "You can't just drag me along. I need to slow down," she insisted.

"Can't," he said. Corbin turned and lifted her into his arms despite her squealing protests and picked up the pace to his waiting SUV. He all but tossed her into the back seat and slid in next to her, pulling her to practically sit on his lap.

"Thank you for doing this for me," she whispered against his neck.

Corbin wrapped his arms around her body. "Honey, you never have to thank me for anything. I did this because I want you in every way possible, Avalon." His voice dripped with innuendo and Ava suddenly felt too hot.

"Where are you taking me?" she questioned.

"Mmm," he hummed. "Remember I told you about a little club in town that I used to go to?" Ava nodded. She remembered thinking that she would kill any sub he took on after her and even having extreme feelings of jealousy that were foreign to her.

Corbin chuckled, "From your murderous expression, you remember it," he said.

"I think I do," she smirked. "You want to go to the

113

club and play with other subs?" Ava asked. She didn't want to admit that she was holding her breath, waiting for him to answer, but she was.

"No," he immediately spat. "I want to go to the club and play with my wife. I might have left out the part about me owning the club," he admitted.

"You own a BDSM club here—in France?" she asked. She sounded more like she was accusing him of something but honestly, she was more shocked than anything else.

"Yep, and as for me wanting to play with other subs, Ava, that isn't going to happen. I only want to play with you. You good with that?" Ava shyly nodded her head.

"Good to know," she teased.

"Now you're just begging to be spanked, aren't you? Between thinking that I'd put my hands on another woman after marrying you and then giving me your sassy backtalk, I think I'm going to need to remind you of rule number five," he said.

"Rule five?" She questioned. Honestly, she had forgotten most of the rules they had made. Corbin told them to her while spanking her ass red and then fucking her. The last thing she remembered from that scene was the rules.

He made a disapproving tsking sound and Ava stifled her giggle. "Yes, rule five—this thing between us is exclusive. I won't touch another woman and you don't get to be with any other man, unless I give permission first." Ava smiled at the thought of being between Corbin and another man. Honestly, she thought the whole thing sounded hot.

"You'd like for me to put you between another Dom and myself, wouldn't you?" he asked.

"I don't know," she stuttered. "Really, I've never done anything like that before but the thought of you doing that with me—to me, makes me hot." She felt crazy admitting something like that to him, but he was her husband now and Ava knew full well Corbin would never let her hide from him.

"Good to know," he teased, giving her own words back to her.

"Any other rules I need to be reminded of?" she sassed.

Corbin reached up under her dress and swatted her bare ass. She intentionally wore no panties because she knew he liked her pussy bare and ready for him. She gasped at the sensation of his big hand rubbing over her sensitive folds.

"I think we should revisit rule number four," he growled.

"Four?" she whispered.

"Yes," he said. "That's the one about me controlling all of your orgasms," he hissed. "It's going to be a damn long time before I give you one," he teased.

"Shit," Ava breathed.

"Yeah, now you're getting the big picture, Wife." He pulled her down for a kiss and Ava knew that she was in for a whole lot of sexual frustration before her new husband finally gave her a release, but it was going to be a hell of a lot of fun in the meantime.

CORBIN

Corbin wasn't sure how he got so lucky with finding Avalon. She was his perfect match and there was no way that he was going to willingly give her up. Sure, the idea of sharing her with another man might be a turn on for them both, but there was no way he was going to let her forget she belonged to him. In fact, tonight he was going to prove that to the whole damn club and if his new wife wanted a third, he knew just the guy to join them. His friend Eric was someone he could trust and Corbin knew he'd be on board for a little fun. He and Eric had played with women before and his friend was fine with being told what to do, usually letting Corbin take lead with everything.

"You have that devilish look on your face that scares me," Ava warned. "Should I be afraid?" That was a very good question and one that Corbin wasn't sure how to answer. Their relationship was so new, he worried that playing with a third might be too much for them.

"Do you trust me?" Corbin questioned.

Ava didn't hesitate, "Yes," she breathed, "with my life." Corbin wasn't sure what he had done to earn her complete trust, but he was sure as hell not going to do anything to hurt what they had built together in such a short amount of time.

"Thank you for that, baby," he said. When the car stopped in front of his club, he got out of the back seat and helped Ava to step free. "If tonight gets to be too much for you, I need you to promise me that you'll use your safe word."

Ava nodded, "Yes, I remember it," she said. Corbin slipped a jewelry box from his jacket pocket. He was going to wait to give it to her but this seemed as good a time as any. "What's this?" Avalon questioned when he handed her the box.

"It's something I'd like you to wear whenever we come to the club to play," he said, suddenly feeling shy. Ava took the box from him and hesitated.

"You've already given me my beautiful wedding ring," she said, holding her hand out to admire the diamond band he had gifted her. Ava opened the jewelry box and gasped. "Ice cream," she whispered. "You gave me my safe word on a collar?"

Corbin nodded, "I had it and your ring both made yesterday, after you agreed to marry me today. I have a local jeweler that does work for me and he was willing to put a rush on the order, for the right price." Corbin pulled the silver choker chain free from the black velvet box and admired the little diamond pendant of an ice cream cone that dangled from the center.

"May I?" He asked.

"Well, it is beautiful," Ava said. "And, I did promise to let you dress me when we go to clubs," she teased, looking up at the massive building that housed his BDSM club. "So, yes," she said, turning away from him to give him better access to her bare neck. He couldn't help himself; Corbin kissed his way down her neck loving the way she shivered against his body and the sexy little sighs she gave him.

"This and your wedding band will be all you wear tonight, Avalon," he whispered into her ear. Her gasp told him that she fully understood his command. She was going to be completely naked while in his club. She was his and it was about time that he showed her and everyone else exactly what that meant.

Corbin fastened the collar around her throat, loving the way it seemed to pinch her skin a little. He knew she had to feel the constraint of the silver chain around her neck and he liked that it would be a constant reminder to Ava who she belonged to.

"Too tight?" he asked.

Ava pressed her fingers against the metal and looked up at him. "No," she said.

"Good, let's go in then," he ordered, holding out his hand for hers. Ava reached for him to let him take her into his club. He nodded to the new woman that sat behind the desk in the lobby. To anyone just happening into the club, it looked like any other business office, but once he led Ava into the main playroom through the heavy wooden doors, it screamed sex club, right down to the velvet red wallpaper.

Ava looked around the room at the various couples

118

that had found quiet corners to play in. "Wow," she breathed. "It's beautiful, Corbin," she said. He shot her a stern look and Ava smiled up at him. "I mean, Sir. It's beautiful, Sir," she corrected.

"Thank you," he said. "It's time to have some fun with my beautiful wife," he said. "You're wearing too many clothes—strip," he ordered. Ava kept her eyes on him and he silently waited her out, ready to dare her to comply, but he watched as Ava did as he asked and by the time she finished stepping free from her wedding gown, all she wore was a sexy smirk that let him know she understood his challenge and she was up for it.

"Good girl," he praised. She bent to remove her heels and he stopped her. "Don't," he ordered. "Leave those on. You will need the height for what I have planned." Ava stood and nodded. She was completely naked; wearing only her new collar, her wedding ring and her sexy, fuck me heels. Corbin was so hard he wasn't sure he was going to be able to keep his promise and hold back her release. He wanted to make tonight last and the only way he was going to be able to do that would be to find his own release.

"On your knees," he commanded. Ava never took her eyes off him, even after they had drawn a small crowd of onlookers to admire her beautiful body. She seemed oblivious to everyone else around them except him. The way she watched him made him even hotter and she knelt in front of him, silently waiting for his next orders.

Corbin pulled his zipper down and let his cock spring free, loving the way Ava licked her lips in anticipation of what he was going to have her do next. "Open," he ordered and she complied. "I need to have an orgasm, baby. It's the only way I will be able to last and make this good for you. I've wanted to fuck you since we left the courthouse," he admitted.

"Yes Sir," Ava said. She wrapped her hands around his shaft and Corbin let her have that control. He loved it when she touched him, seeming to need more of what he was giving her. It was as if she needed all of him and he wanted to give Ava that but he worried that he didn't know how. He watched as her tongue darted out of her mouth and licked the head of his cock, causing it to jump.

"Fuck," he spat. "Stop playing with me, Ava. Get me off," he ordered. She smiled and sucked him into her mouth, knowing exactly what she was doing to him and how she was driving him to the edge. Corbin took control of her mouth, pulling her hair back so he could watch his cock as he used her mouth to pump in and out. He took what he needed from her and when she let him slide to the back of her throat and swallowed around him, he lost himself into her mouth. Ava took everything he gave her and licked his cock clean. When she finished, she sat back on her heels and looked up at him, a proud smile on her face.

"Vixen," he taunted. Ava giggled and took the hand he offered to help her off the floor.

"I just did as you asked, Sir," she teased.

"You never do as I ask, Wife," he said. "But you will." Corbin spotted Eric in the corner of the room, surrounded by a few women he didn't seem much interested in and nodded for him to join them.

"Up on the bench," Corbin ordered.

Ava climbed up onto the spanking bench gifting him with a glorious view of her ass. "That's perfect, honey," he praised. Corbin stripped out of his shirt and jacket, wearing just his trousers and turned to find Eric eyeing Ava. Corbin shook his friend's hand and nodded to where Ava was perched on the bench, still assuming the position he ordered her into.

"My wife," he said, nodding to her. "You want to give us a hand tonight?"

"Wife?" Eric asked. "Congrats, man," he offered. Eric was always a big draw to the local French BDSM scene. The women really loved American men and Eric Balthazar was as American as they came. The French women fell for his long blond hair and baby blue eyes that fit perfectly with his Southern California appeal.

Corbin could tell that Ava was listening to everything they were saying and judging by the look of panic in her eyes, he was going to have to do some convincing and fast if they were going to get their chance to play with Eric.

"You trust me, baby?" Corbin asked again. This time, he could feel Ava's hesitation. "You say your safe word and this all ends, here and now," he promised. He meant it too. Corbin wouldn't do anything to push Ava into something she wasn't ready for. "If you don't want to play with a third, then we don't." Ava looked over her shoulder to Eric, as if sizing him up.

"Hi," Eric said, giving a little wave.

"Hey," Ava whispered. She looked back up at Corbin and sighed. "Who do I take orders from?" she asked.

Corbin stroked a hand down her face and cupped her jaw. "Me and only me. I'm your Dom and your husband. You will never take orders from anyone else, understand?" Corbin knew he sounded like a possessive ass but he didn't care.

"Yes Sir," she stuttered. "I want to play," she said.

"We will take this slow tonight," he offered. Ava nodded and he tossed Eric a leather flogger. "She likes it rough," Corbin said. "Just her ass," he added. Eric nodded, knowing just what to do. That was the main reason Corbin had chosen him to play—he knew and trusted Eric and he wouldn't let just anyone touch his wife.

Corbin sat in front of Avalon, watching her beautiful face as his friend marked her ass with the leather flogger. She was so expressive and he could tell the exact moment she started to slip into sub space. She was gorgeous to watch and the very last thing he wanted to do was deny her the release she so desperately needed.

Eric landed the final blow and Ava cried out and moaned. "Please," she whimpered.

"Roll over and let your legs spill over the sides of the bench," Corbin ordered. I want to see how wet your pussy is, baby and then I'm going to let Eric have a taste of just what his spanking did to you." Ava whimpered and Corbin waited her out, hoping like hell she didn't use her safe word. She nodded and did as he asked.

"Like this?" she questioned.

"Yes, my beautiful wife, just like that," Corbin

praised. He nodded over to Eric who seemed to be eagerly waiting for his next set of instructions. From the erection he was sporting, Corbin could tell his friend needed to get off.

"You can taste her but that will be it for tonight," Corbin said. Eric nodded and smiled down at Ava, spreading her legs further open to inspect her drenched folds.

"She's so fucking wet, man," Eric groaned. Corbin had called one of Eric's groupies over and whispered into her ear. The little blonde smiled and nodded and went to stand beside Eric, just as Corbin had ordered.

"Steph wants to give you a blow job while you eat my wife's pussy," Corbin offered. The little blonde vixen coyly smiled and nodded. When she sank to her knees and sucked Eric into her mouth, Corbin knew his friend wouldn't last long.

He stood over Ava and watched as Eric licked his way into her pussy, causing her to buck and squirm on the small leather bench. "Hold still, honey," Corbin ordered. "Let Eric taste you and then I'm going to fuck you until you are shouting my name," he promised.

"Yes, Sir," she breathed. "I need you, Corbin," she begged. He kissed his way down her body, giving each one of her breasts special attention, knowing that she was on edge from what he and Eric were working together to do to her.

Corbin worked his way back up her body and kissed his way into her mouth and when he knew she couldn't take anymore, he told her to come for him and she did. She squirmed and thrashed against Eric's mouth and

Corbin was sure he had never seen anything so beautiful in his life.

Eric finished lapping up Ava's release and stood, pulling his cock free from Steph's mouth and jerking himself off onto the blonde sub's pretty breasts. Steph smiled up at Eric triumphantly and he helped her to stand. "Get a room with me?" he asked and the blonde nodded. He nodded at Corbin on his way out of the playroom and gave one last look back at Ava.

"Was that alright?" Ava stood and nervously tried to cover her body with her arms.

Corbin tugged her against his body. "It was more than alright," he admitted. "I loved watching you and sharing you with another man. I liked knowing that he wanted what is mine but he could never really have you because I own you, Ava—body, mind and soul."

Ava nodded and Corbin worried that he had pushed her too hard. "Tell me you are alright," he ordered.

"I think I am," she admitted and gave him her sweet smile. "I liked it too, knowing that you were in complete control and wouldn't let anything go too far."

"Always," he promised.

AVALON

They spent the next week in France and most of that time was spent in bed or at the club. Ava was beginning to get the full gist of just how demanding Corbin was going to be and she had to admit, she loved every minute.

Her business partner had given her some much needed time off to spend with her new husband as a wedding gift. Today was her first full day back at work on the new line and she used her time to daydream about her husband. Her blissfully happy mood lasted until Zara called to say she was in labor and heading to the hospital. As soon as she hung up with her best friend, Corbin called to tell her that Aiden had phoned to tell him the baby was on the way. He had sent word to his pilot to have his jet ready for them and with any luck, they would get home in time to welcome the new addition to their little makeshift family.

A part of her was worried about what their lives were going to look like once they got back to the States.

They really hadn't made plans and were basically living day to day, but going home was going to prove challenging, especially since they hadn't even discussed where they were going to live.

Corbin rushed into the bedroom where she was packing her bags for their trip home and he looked just as frazzled and excited as she felt. He kissed her cheek and grabbed his own suitcase.

"You ready to be an aunt?" Corbin questioned.

Honestly, she was. Ava had been excited about Zara's little one since the day she announced she was pregnant. What she wouldn't admit to was the fact that every time she saw her best friend, she felt a pang of jealousy and a strange longing for something she thought she never wanted. When she was growing up, the thought of someday meeting a man, falling in love and having a family never crossed her mind. After her mother died and her brother disappeared, she decided to follow her dreams and go into fashion. Her grandfather convinced her to take the leap and invested in her company and she was able to make him proud of all her achievements before he passed away. That was enough for her until she met Corbin.

He made her feel things she didn't plan on feeling and want things she never would have guessed were possible. "I am," she admitted. "I already love Zara's baby, so much," she said.

"I know how you feel. When Lucy and Laney were born, I wasn't very impressed by the little people taking my best friend away from me. But spending time with them—well, let's just say that I've had a change of heart.

Those little girls are pretty damn awesome," he admitted. Ava watched as Corbin threw his clothes into his suitcase, not bothering to fold them and shook her head.

"What?" he asked.

"You really are a crappy packer," she teased. "Here, let me help." She took his shirt from his hands and took over packing for him, neatly folding his now wrinkled clothing.

Corbin wrapped his arms around her from behind and kissed her neck. "You know, I could get used to my wife taking care of me," he admitted.

Ava giggled, "I'm pretty sure that was a part of our vows," she teased.

"You mean you vowed to pack for me?" he asked. Ava swatted him away and tried to pretend to be upset by the idea of having to pack for him even though she wasn't.

"Have you ever thought about having kids of your own?" Ava questioned.

"No," Corbin said. He didn't seem to hesitate with his answer and Ava didn't try to hide her disappointment. "I never thought about having kids before," he added. "Well, before I met you. Now, it's all I can think about and everything I want for us." Ava smiled up at him and he pulled her into his arms.

"Really?" she asked.

Corbin smiled, "How about you? You ever thought of having a few rugrats?"

Ava nodded, "I always put my career first, but ever since Zara told me that she was pregnant, it's been in

the back of my mind. I think I'd like to have kids—
someday." She knew that they were nowhere near ready
to talk about having a baby, but she liked the idea of
them revisiting the whole subject when things calmed
down.

"Someday it is then," Corbin agreed. "Now get a
move on, Wife. We have a plane to catch and a new baby
to meet." Ava hesitated and Corbin seemed to notice.
"What's wrong?" he asked.

Ava shrugged, "I'm just worried about what happens
next," she admitted.

"I thought we just covered that," Corbin said.

"Sure," she agreed. "But, I'm talking about after we
fly home and meet the baby. What happens then?
Where will we live?" Corbin gently kissed her lips and
she snuggled into his hold. What was it about this man
that made her feel that everything was going to be
alright no matter how messed up things were?

"Honey, we can live wherever you'd like. Your townhouse, my penthouse—hell, I'll buy you a new house
and we can live there." Ava rolled her eyes and giggled.

"I think we can make do with one of our houses,
Corbin."

"Great, then move in with me. My penthouse is
bigger and closer to both of our offices." The thought
of giving up her beloved townhouse made her heart
ache a little. That place was home for both her and
Zara for so many years. They got through college
together in that house. They had parties, movie
marathons, and stayed up all night to talk about boys
in that little townhome. Sure, Zara wasn't moving

back in and Ava was left to live alone but it was still hers.

"You're making this more difficult than it is, baby," Corbin said. "I'll move into your place, if that will make you happy. What do you want, Ava?" That was a good question and one that she didn't want to think too long on. She already had what she really wanted—him. He was right, where they lived didn't matter.

"I'll move into your place and put my townhouse on the market," she said. "You're right—it doesn't matter where we live and your penthouse has more space than my tiny townhouse."

"Say that again," he prompted.

"Your place has more room?" Ava questioned.

"No, the part about me being right," he teased.

Ava giggled. "Fine—you're right, Corbin," she said. He practically gloated, smiling down at her as if he had just won a contest.

"You'll find that I'm right a lot of the time, Ava," he boasted. She rolled her eyes and finished throwing the last of her things into her suitcase.

"Ready?" Corbin asked, holding out his hand for her.

"Yep," she said, taking it. Ava knew she was being silly but she felt sadness about having to leave France. It was as if she and Corbin had built their own personal little world and they were leaving it to return to what was certain to be utter chaos. But there would be no hiding from reality—it was waiting for them and it was time to face it but this time, she wouldn't be alone. This time, she'd have Corbin by her side.

CORBIN

They got home just in time to meet their niece and Corbin had to admit that watching Ava holding a newborn did strange things to his heart. It made him feel things he wasn't sure he'd ever feel and that made him a little nervous.

As soon as Ava agreed to move into his place, he set the wheels in motion, calling his mother to enlist her help. Rose was all too happy to lend a hand in planning the move and even had the moving company at Ava's place before their plane landed the next morning. He knew he was rushing things but he wouldn't take the chance that she would change her mind. Besides, that seemed to be how this whole thing between the two of them worked—fast. Ever since their first night together at the club, he couldn't seem to slow things down and honestly, he didn't want to.

As soon as they landed, he called Aiden to get an update and he told them that they had a little girl and were naming her Lexi Avalon. Corbin didn't miss the way Ava teared up hearing that they named the baby after her.

When they finally got to the hospital, she and Zara acted as if they hadn't spoken every day on the phone or video chatted every chance they got. Ava gushed about how perfect the newest addition was and Corbin had to agree that she was pretty awesome. But when Ava took the baby from Zara, his heart stuttered and all their talk about having kids "someday" went right out the window. All he wanted was to convince his new wife that they should start working on expanding their family now, but he worried that she wasn't ready for that big of a step.

First, he needed to get her settled in his penthouse and then they could sort out this mess with her father. Ava's birthday was just around the corner and it was about time he met the man who was trying to hurt the woman he loved. They needed to get a few things straight and then he was going to take great pleasure in watching as Ava gave him the news that she was married and would be keeping her inheritance. Not that any of that mattered to him. Corbin didn't marry Ava for her to be able to keep her money. He didn't give one fuck about how much money she had. Hell, she now had access to everything he had and that was enough for them both and their future generations. He married Ava because he was in love with her and the thought of her walking away from him, to marry someone else, just pissed him off. He couldn't let that happen.

By the time they got back to his place, he knew Ava had to be exhausted but the movers were there, bringing in the last of her things. Rose was bossing them around, just like she had him when he was a little boy. God, he missed his mother while he was away.

As soon as they walked into the penthouse, Rose shooed them right back out the front door. "Out," she shouted.

"Ma," he protested. "What the hell?"

"Don't you Ma me," she shot back. "You carry your new bride over the threshold of your first home together or you'll have bad luck," she insisted. Ava giggled and looked at him expectantly. Corbin dropped both of their suitcases in the front hallway and lifted her into his arms. She breathlessly looked up at him and he couldn't help himself, he kissed her and by the time he finished, he was feeling a little breathless himself. Rose cleared her throat, reminding him that she was still waiting on him to follow tradition and carry Ava across the threshold.

He stepped into his foyer, holding Ava against his chest and shot his mother a condescending look. "How about now, Ma?" Corbin questioned. "Will we have better luck now?"

His mother shook her head at him. "It's like someone else raised you, Corbin James," she teased. He put Ava down and pulled his mom in for a quick hug.

"You raised me, Mom and you did a fantastic job, even if I do say so myself," Corbin boasted. Ava and Rose both broke down in fits of laughter and he didn't hide his smile. He loved to hear them both laughing together; he wanted so much for them to get along. They were the two most important women in his life and the fact that they seemed to like each other helped him to relax some.

Rose hugged Ava and welcomed her into the family. They talked about where the movers had put most of her stuff and then slid right into chatting about the ceremony and France. After a good thirty minutes had passed, Corbin gave up trying to find a place in their conversation and went to find a takeout menu for his favorite Asian place. He ordered them all dinner and found a bottle of wine to go with their meal. When he returned to the family room to find them, Rose and Ava were huddled together on his sectional, still gabbing about their trip.

"So, you liked the house in France then?" Rose questioned when Ava told her that Corbin had moved her into his French home. It was silly that it mattered to him, but he was curious to hear her answer. He wanted her to feel at home in all his places.

"I loved it," she gushed. Corbin found himself breathing a sigh of relief and his mother looked up at him, her smile seemed to be permanently plastered on her beautiful face. He knew that Rose always wanted him to settle down, but every time she brought up the topic of him finding a nice girl, he'd quickly change the subject. His poor mother must have thought he wasn't ever going to settle down and find someone, yet here they were, talking about houses and surprise weddings.

"I hope you don't mind me taking the initiative to move you in here so quickly," Rose said. Ava reached across the seat and took Rose's hand.

"Of course not," she said. "I appreciate everything you are doing for me, Rose," Ava said.

Rose nodded, "How about you call me Mom?" she asked. Ava didn't answer at first and Corbin worried that his mother's request had been too much for her. He knew that Ava's own mother passed away when she was little and maybe calling her that would bring back bad memories.

"No, never mind," Rose said, probably picking up on Ava's indecision. "Forget I mentioned it. I guess I'm just so happy to have you in our little family," Rose admitted. "I just got carried away."

"It's alright," Ava said. "It's just that I haven't called anyone that for a long time. My own mother died when I was very young and well—I'd love to call you 'Mom', Rose," she said. Rose pulled Ava in for a side hug and Corbin moaned.

"You alright, son?" Rose questioned.

"You two are mushier than a sappy card commercial," he grumbled, causing them both to laugh.

"Well, I feel very fortunate that my son has finally taken my advice and found someone to settle down and be happy with," Rose said. "I'm just hoping that I don't have to wait too long to be a grandma," she admitted.

"Don't push, Ma," Corbin warned. "How about you practice on Aiden's three girls and let me and Ava get adjusted to married life first?"

Rose nodded. "Sorry," she said more to Ava than to him. "I guess I have baby fever after getting to meet little Lexi today."

"Oh—I feel the same way. She's beautiful, isn't she?" Ava asked.

"Yeah, thank God she looks like Zara and not Aiden," Corbin butted in.

"Corbin James," Rose chided. "Aiden is a good looking man and your best friend."

"I haven't forgotten that, Ma," Corbin said. "But, he'd make one ugly girl."

"So, what's next for you two newlyweds?" Rose questioned. "Have you met Ava's family yet, Corbin?" Ava shot him a pleading look and he smiled and winked.

"Nope, but I have a feeling that I will be meeting her dad real soon," he admitted. Ava rolled her eyes and he laughed.

"Well, I'm sure he will be just as thrilled about the two of you getting married as I am," Rose said.

"I doubt that, but thanks, Ma," Corbin said. The doorbell rang and he thanked his lucky stars for the interruption. The last thing he wanted to do was explain to his mother about the stipulations of Ava's inheritance or the fact that she had to get married. She was his now and nothing else mattered.

AVALON

Ava walked into the kitchen and flopped down into a chair. She hated that she was going to have to face her father so soon after returning home but there would be no avoiding him. Ava counted herself lucky that her father had waited at least a few days to demand her presence, after she and Corbin had returned home to the States. But, he wasn't about to let her birthday pass without seeing for himself if she was truly married or not. Ava told her father that she had 'news' to share with him but left it at that. And now, she had been summoned to his home. Her dear old dad was sure to add the fact that he was quite willing to call in his team of lawyers to force her to accept his invitation, if necessary. He could do it too and that thought alone had Ava seeing red.

When her grandfather gave her dad permission to alter his will, to add the stipulation that Avalon would have to forfeit her inheritance if she wasn't married by age thirty, he also allowed for her father to be made executor of his estate. That meant her father could challenge her marriage to Corbin and there would be nothing she could do about it. There were built in safety nets in her grandfather's will that also permitted both Ava and her new husband to be extensively questioned if there was any plausibility of their marriage not being legal. The document was legal—iron- clad in fact. Corbin had his personal lawyers go over the will, but she knew that whoever was going to be investigating them, on her father's behalf, would be sticking his or her nose into their business. They would be asking private questions that Ava would rather not have to answer and the thought of putting Corbin through any of this infuriated her. A family reunion was the very last thing she wanted on her birthday. Honestly, she wanted to spend her thirtieth birthday cuddled up with Corbin in bed but now that plan was shot to hell.

"What has you in such a lovely mood, Princess?" Corbin teased. Ava huffed out her breath and shot him a look to let him know she was not in the mood for his teasing. "Whoa, honey," he said, holding up his hands as if in surrender. "It was just a question. Geeze Ava, what's going on?"

"My father is what's going on," she admitted. "I received a phone call this afternoon and I have been summoned to his home for dinner tonight," she moaned. "I just wanted a quiet evening with you for my birthday and now we have to see my father."

"I think you mean to say that 'we' have been summoned because we're a team now—remember? I can tell you I don't really do well with taking orders. I'm more of a give the orders type of guy," Corbin said, bobbing his eyebrows at her. Ava couldn't help but giggle. He was always doing that for her—making bad situations better and taking care of her, even when she was acting like a miserable cow. "But I'm sure I can think of a few ways to salvage your birthday, baby. How about we go to dinner after our visit and then come back here so I can worship that sexy birthday suit of yours." Ava giggled again, loving the way he couldn't seem to keep his mind or hands off her body.

"Thanks," she said.

"For?" he asked.

"For always making me feel better." Ava stood and crossed the room to where Corbin sat. She didn't wait or even hesitate, just crawled into his lap and snuggled against his body.

"We have to go. It's part of the stipulation with my grandfather's will. We will need to not only prove that we are legally married, but we will most likely have to answer questions that will be personal or even private. My father will leave no stone unturned when it comes to trying to prove that we aren't legally married. If he can prove that we are married just so I can collect the rest of my inheritance, I'm screwed."

"Except he won't be able to prove that because it isn't true—right, Ava?" Corbin questioned. He looked downright angry and Ava thought back over her words trying to figure out where she had gone wrong.

"That's not what I meant, Corbin," she defended.

"We might have started out that way but you have to know that isn't how I feel about you or our marriage now," Corbin said. "This isn't a marriage of convenience for me, Ava. I didn't marry you for you to be able to keep your damn money. Hell, I have enough of my own and now, what's mine is yours."

"No, Corbin," she whispered. "I don't want your money. I want what is mine and I won't just let my father waltz into my life and take it away from me. I appreciate that you want to take care of me but that isn't necessary. We just need to get through this next part and then I'll have my inheritance back and won't need your money."

"Is that all this is to you, Ava?" Corbin asked. "Am I just a way for you to get your money back? Is our marriage just one big scam to you?" He sounded as if he was accusing her of something awful but he wasn't completely wrong. This thing between the two of them might have started as a way for her to keep her inheritance but it ended up being so much more.

"No," she admitted. "At first, I took you up on your offer so I'd be able to keep my money, but it's turned into so much more, Corbin." Ava took a deep breath. It was now or never and she had always been a rip the band-aid off quickly, kind of girl.

"I've told you that I'm falling for you but what if that isn't completely true?" she asked.

"So this has all been a ruse? You don't have feelings for me?" Ava wasn't sure which hurt more—Corbin's anger or the hurt she could hear in his voice.

"No. I guess I'm not explaining any of this right," she mumbled. "I'm in love with you, Corbin," she admitted. He opened his mouth as if he wanted to say something and then seemed to decide against it and quickly pressed his lips together. They sat in silence for what felt like forever. Ava hated that she just blurted out how she felt about him with no warning or pretense.

"Say something," she begged. "Anything."

"What do you want for me to say here, Ava?" Corbin asked. "Do you want me to say that I'm in love with you too and I've been waiting to hear you admit how you felt for weeks now?"

"Only if that is what you are really feeling," she said.

Corbin nodded and smiled. "It is," he said. "I'm in love with you too, Ava. Hell, maybe I have been since we took Laney and Lucy for ice cream, all those months ago—I don't know. What I do know is that I'm head over heels for you and that isn't going to ever change."

"But, my father," she started to protest, but Corbin put his big hand over her mouth, effectively stopping her from saying anything else.

"Your father can come for us and we'll be ready. We know the basics and we'll just have to learn the rest. For now, we'll get dressed and go see what your father wants, but we won't be having dinner with him. I've already planned a birthday dinner for my new wife. If your dad decides to pursue questioning us, he'll have to do it another day," he assured. Ava just wished she could bottle some of his enthusiasm because she wasn't quite so sure of everything. What she was sure of was that her father was probably up to no good and she was madly in love with her new husband.

※

Corbin had his driver bring the car around to pick them up and Ava was glad that he wasn't driving them to her father's house. This way he could sit in the back seat with her and offer her the comfort she so desperately needed. As usual, he seemed to sense just what she needed and as soon as he slid into the back seat, Corbin pulled her onto his lap.

"You know we don't have to do this. I can have my lawyers deal with this whole mess and we can avoid your father all together," Corbin offered. Ava wished that could be true but she knew her father—he'd find a way to get to her. He seemed to take some sick pleasure in making her squirm and Ava knew the sooner they got this visit over with, the better.

"No, I can handle this. Besides, I have my birthday dinner to look forward to after this is all over," she said. Corbin had promised her a night out at her favorite restaurant in town and then they'd spend the rest of the night in bed, if she had any say in the matter.

"And, don't forget the part about me taking you home and the whole matter of body worshipping," he teased. Ava wrapped her arms around his broad shoulders and pulled him in for a kiss.

"I don't think I could forget that part," she admitted. "In fact, it's all I can think about."

Corbin kissed his way down the column of her neck. "How long will it take us to get to your father's house?" He whispered into her ear, causing her to shiver. God, she wished she could lie and tell him that they had enough time to do everything that his sexy voice told her he wanted to do with her, but they didn't. Her two worlds were about to collide. Honestly, she was shocked that Corbin and her father lived so close to each other but had never run into the other. They even ran in the same elite circles, but knowing her father, he wouldn't have given Corbin Eklund a second glance knowing that he wasn't from old money.

Her father used to like to remind her that there were two types of rich men—those from old money like him and those that made their fortune on their own. For some reason, her father looked down at the men who worked hard for every penny—men like Corbin. Maybe it was because he was simply handed everything in life but she had a deep respect for people who worked for what they had. She appreciated the money she had made on her own in the fashion industry so much more than the money her family had given her.

"Not far," she answered. "My father lives just around the corner from your building."

Corbin groaned his frustration and she giggled. "Then let's get this fucking meeting over with so we can go to dinner and I can get you home," he said. "I want to play." Hearing Corbin admit that he wanted her made her feel as though she might self-combust.

"Deal," she quickly agreed just as the car pulled up in front of her father's place. She looked at the house that she once thought of as home and felt nothing. It was crazy that she once happily lived there with her mother, brother and father and now they were all gone—well except her dad but he wasn't the same man she once knew. She felt a deep sadness every time she had to go to that house now and Ava hated that she was dragging Corbin into this mess with her.

"You don't have to do this," she offered. "You can back out now and no one will ever have to know that you married me." Ava looked up at Corbin and saw every ounce of his anger staring back at her.

"Now I think you're just trying to piss me off, honey. I've already told you that I didn't marry you to save your inheritance. I'm in love with you and if you try to give me a fucking out again, I'll spank your ass red and you won't be able to sit down for weeks." She nodded, knowing that her bossy husband meant every word of his threat.

"Okay," she whispered. "I just feel like I'm piling a lot on you and we're still technically newlyweds."

"Then let's start acting like fucking newlyweds," he growled, pulling Ava down onto his body and sealing his lips over hers. He kissed her for so long, she forgot all about being parked in front of her father's house until a sharp rapping sound on the back window got their attention. Corbin rolled down the window and looked out at her very angry father who was standing on the curb, watching them.

"What the hell is going on here?" he asked.

"Dad," Ava coldly greeted him.

"You want to explain what you are doing making out in the back of a car while parked in front of my house, Avalon?" Her father seemed more than angry; he was downright pissed. She hadn't gotten around to telling her dad that she was married. Really, Ava wanted to see the look on his face when she broke the news. All she disclosed was that she was seeing someone and that she wanted to bring him by to meet her father. Of course, he reluctantly agreed and demanded that she come over to sign the final papers from her grandfather's will. If she was a betting woman, she'd put money on her father already believing that he had won in this whole game he was playing. What he didn't know was that she was holding a trump card and she was about to play it.

"Well, Dad," she started but before she could get the rest out, Corbin squeezed her hand to let her know that he had it. She looked up at him, smiled and nodded, giving him the go ahead.

"I was kissing my wife," Corbin said.

"Your wife?" her father stuttered.

"Yes, Dad," Ava confirmed. "Corbin and I have been married for a few weeks now." The look on his face was almost comical and she was doing everything in her power not to burst out into fits of laughter.

"Married," her father said again.

"Yep," Corbin said. "Married."

"I'm assuming that's why you summoned me here, Dad," Ava asked. "Did you find out that I had a new boyfriend and never assumed that we'd taken the next step? What did you have planned? Were you going to rub it in my face that I didn't meet my deadline? Did you want to size up the man that I am with—because he's quite impressive," she admitted.

"Aw, thanks, babe," Corbin said, giving her another quick kiss.

"So, which was it going to be, Dad?" she asked again. Her father didn't answer and she knew that her hunch was correct. He had already taken a victory lap and now he was clueless as to what to do next. She almost felt bad for her father—almost.

"Were you going to even wish me a happy birthday?" Ava questioned.

"As you've already guessed, this wasn't about your birthday—this is business, Avalon and you know how I handle business." She knew exactly how her father handled his business and people he considered threats to him and his interests. She and Corbin's challenge now presented a threat to him and Ava knew to watch her back.

"How about we go into the house and discuss this like civilized adults," Corbin offered.

"Really, there isn't much more to talk about, Mr.—" Her father looked at him as if he was trying to size Corbin up.

"Corbin Eklund," he said, opening his door to stand. Corbin held out his hand for her father and she could tell by his wide-eyed expression that he wasn't planning on her new husband being quite so big. Again, Ava had to fight the urge to giggle.

"Ronald Michaels," her father said, shaking Corbin's extended hand. "You know this changes nothing, right Avalon?" he said, looking around Corbin to where she still sat in the back of the car. "You will have to prove that your marriage isn't a sham and I will make sure that my lawyers leave no rock unturned in the process of proving you a liar."

Corbin stepped in front of her father's sight line to her and squared his shoulders. Ava was behind him, but she knew what her husband looked like when he was pissed off and she also knew her father might be afraid of him but he'd never back down.

"From now on, Mr. Michaels, when you have something to say to my wife, it will go through me or my lawyers. You will find that I have just as many resources as you do and I will protect what's mine. Avalon is now mine and you will do well to remember that," Corbin growled. He turned and slid back into the car and pulled her against his body, shutting his window. Corbin gave the driver directions to the restaurant and they left—just like that. There were no further arguments or fanfare that usually occurred when she tried to put her foot down with her father. They simply pulled away from the curb and she didn't even bother to look back to where they had left her dad. She knew all too well that she'd find him watching them drive off, a mean scowl on his face. But this time, she didn't worry about what he could do to her or what her next move should be. She had Corbin by her side, holding her protectively against his body, and that was all she needed.

CORBIN

After a quiet dinner, Corbin took Avalon home and had plans to tie her to their bed, but as soon as they entered the building, he and Ava were immediately ushered into a small office by the head of his security.

"You mind telling me what the hell is going on here, Rob?" Corbin questioned. "It's Ava's birthday and I'd like to get on with celebrating with my new wife."

"Sorry Mr. Eklund, Mrs. Eklund," Rob nodded at Ava and tried to smile, but Corbin could see the concern behind the older man's eyes. "We've had a security breach and our team hasn't finished sweeping the penthouse yet," Rob said.

"What the fuck do you mean by security breach?" Corbin growled.

"Housekeeping saw a man in the elevator on their way out and he got away before they could report him. He apparently gained access to your penthouse and we're not sure how. We were given a good description and the team is working on pulling up video footage to see if we can get a picture of him. Don't worry, Sir, we will find him and figure out why he was here."

"Make sure you do," Corbin said. "I won't have my wife put in danger. We are going to stay elsewhere tonight. I'll be in touch and have one of the guys bring us some things we will need." The idea of staying at the penthouse while someone was lurking outside their front door made him half crazy. Ava had been through enough crap with her father; he couldn't let someone else completely ruin her birthday.

"We can go back to my townhouse," she offered. "It's still on the market and there is enough furniture there that we would be comfortable."

"Your security is basically non-existent, Mrs. Eklund," Rob cut in before Corbin could veto her idea. His head of security was right, she had awful security measures in place and there would be no way to keep her safe there.

"Okay, then what are our options?" Ava asked. Corbin hated the defeat in her voice.

"I own a hotel on the outskirts of town. It has fantastic security and I'll be able to keep you safe there," Corbin said. He wrapped his arms around her and she shivered. "I'm sorry about all of this, baby. I hate that this is ruining your birthday."

"Corbin, no," she said. "You aren't responsible for any of this. Being with you has only made my birthday all that more special."

"I'm sure I can do better once we get to my suite at the hotel," he whispered into her ear.

"Keep this between us and the team, Rob. I don't

want this leaking to the press," Corbin ordered. His head of security nodded and promised to keep him updated when they had more information.

"I'll contact you as soon as we have a clear image of the guy," Rob agreed. Corbin nodded and ushered Ava out of the security office and into his private elevator that would take them back down to the garage.

"Are we safe?" Ava stuttered. "You know without your security?"

Corbin hated the fear he heard in her voice. "Yeah, baby," he said. "I have two guys waiting for us in the garage and my driver. They will tail us to my hotel to make sure we aren't being followed. I won't let anyone touch you, Ava." He wrapped a protective arm around her body and she snuggled into his side, seeming to need his comfort.

"Thank you, Corbin," she whispered. The elevator doors opened and they were immediately flanked by two of his security detail. He wasn't taking any chances with his wife. When Aiden was running for the Senate, they decided to up their security measures for both of their families and that included Rose. Corbin and Aiden weren't going to take any chances with the people they loved. They quickly found out that there were a lot of people in the world who wanted to get to them just because of who they were and the company they built. Now that Ava was in his life, he appreciated the security team even more. He'd do just about anything to keep his wife safe.

They stepped out of the elevator, his arm still protectively around Ava's body and he didn't miss her little gasp when she realized that his security team was by their sides. "Is this all really necessary?" she asked.

"Yep," he said. "I won't take chances with you, honey. Once we are at the hotel and I go over the security plans with my team there, I'll make this all up to you." He playfully bobbed his eyebrows at her, hoping to alleviate some of the stress he himself was feeling. He knew that people would try to get to them—they were one powerful couple with his money and her name, but he didn't like the fact that someone was actually in their home. That was the last straw for him and he would make sure that never happened again.

"I'm sure you will," she whispered. Corbin helped her slip into the back seat of the waiting SUV and slid in next to her. "How long until we are at the hotel?" she nervously asked.

"Not too long," he said. "You just relax and let me worry about everything."

"I just think that it's a crazy coincidence that this guy broke into our home after we had our meeting with my father today," she whispered.

"Are you accusing your dad of breaking into our place, Ava?" Corbin asked. Honestly, he had the same suspicions, but he didn't want to outright accuse her father or anything like that. He wouldn't put it past the guy though. From their earlier exchange, her father wasn't too happy with Ava and her decision to marry him. Corbin wasn't sure how a man could have so much contempt for his own child but that was always something that haunted him. His own father walked away from him and his mother before he was even born and he always wondered how a man could do that. He had thought about Ava pregnant with his child a half dozen times, since getting back and meeting Aiden and Zara's little one, and each and every time his damn heart felt as if it would burst in his chest. If he was ever given the privilege of having kids with Ava, he wouldn't fuck it up.

"I think it's a good possibility that he had something to do with the break- in. But why would he go to such lengths to get to me? Was anything taken?" she asked. That was the part that had Corbin stumped—nothing seemed to be touched.

"No," he breathed. "It was as if he didn't touch anything. He must have been wearing gloves too because my team found no trace of prints." Corbin wished he had more information, but he knew his security team was the best his money could buy and if there was something to be found, they'd find it.

"Then, why go to the trouble of breaking into our place?" Ava asked. Corbin shrugged, not really having an answer to give her.

"We'll know more soon, honey," he promised.

"I need for you to tell me what you find, Corbin," she insisted. He worried that she'd ask that of him. He was hoping to keep her safe from this mess. If there was an issue with her father, he wanted to handle it for her, but he also knew his wife and Ava would give him hell for keeping her in the dark. "Corbin," she warned, when he didn't immediately give her an answer.

"Fine," he reluctantly agreed. "I'll keep you up to speed but you won't be getting involved in this, Ava. If something needs to be handled—even something involving your father, I'll be the one doing it. Agreed?" Corbin waited her out, knowing that she wanted to give him some fight just from the expression on her beautiful face.

"Fine," she said.

"Thank you for that, honey," he said, kissing the top of her head. Ava snuggled into his body and he wrapped an arm around Ava's waist. She yawned and he knew it had been a long day for her. "Get some shut eye," he ordered. "I'll wake you when we get to the hotel."

Ava nodded and yawned again and before he knew it, his girl was softly snoring on his shoulder. Corbin smiled to himself, loving the fact that she felt so comfortable around him, letting him see all of her and he had to admit, he loved every part of Avalon Eklund— especially her new last name.

They spent two long days cooped up in his suite at the hotel he owned across town. He had kept Ava occupied in his bed, but he could tell that his new wife was getting a little antsy. If he was being honest, he was starting to feel the exact same way, but there was no way Ava would let him leave the hotel without her and taking her out into public without knowing who or what the threat was yet, wasn't acceptable.

Corbin had called Aiden to warn him about what was going on. They couldn't rule out the possibility that whoever was in his penthouse, two nights prior, wasn't there for Avalon but for him. He and Aiden had faced a few security breaches in their time, especially owning a multi-billion dollar business. Hell, he had faced his share of surprise visits from women admirers who wanted a piece of him, but this was different. He couldn't explain it, but this time his gut was screaming at him that Ava was the target and he would do everything in his power to keep his wife safe.

Aiden agreed with him, but also took measures to protect his family. Zara kept the girls home from school and Aiden had taken up residence in his family room, turning it into a makeshift office. Corbin had done the same at his hotel and even had Ava's business partner send over her laptop and some work she could do from the hotel. She was supposed to travel back to France in a week, but there was no way he was going to let that happen—not until they knew who or what was after them.

Corbin looked across the room to find Ava hard at work on her computer and the way she was biting her bottom lip into her sexy mouth, as if deep in thought, was completely turning him on. "I can feel you looking at me," she said, not looking up from her laptop. "And I can't. I'm working."

"You could, if I ordered you to," he countered. Ava shot him a sexy smile and rolled her eyes.

"I'll make you a deal. You let me go to France next week and I'll stop working to meet your demands," she sassed. It was a tempting offer but he also knew that letting Ava out of his sight wasn't an option. There was no way he would agree to let her go to France next week.

"No," he said, pointing a finger in her direction. She made a humphing noise and stuck her nose back into her computer screen. Her adorable, sultry pout was nearly his undoing. "It's just not safe," Ava," he amended.

"How am I any safer here, trapped in this hotel room with you and your security team stationed outside in the hallway? We can just bring them along and they can guard the house in France," she offered. They had already been over all of this though and he had a feeling that his wife would continue to push until she got her way.

"I told you I don't have time to go to France and you're not going without me," Corbin grumbled. "I won't change my mind on this, Ava." She crossed her arms over her impressive cleavage and it was all he could do to keep his wits about him.

"I need to get out of this hotel room, Corbin. Take me to the club—we'd be safe there and we can play," she offered. Now, that sounded like a fucking fantastic idea but he also knew it was a bad one.

"You know that your father is a member there and he has friends in high places. If he's the one trying to get to us, we would be giving him easy access." Corbin had done a little digging around at the club and he had found that Ronald Michaels' reach was far and wide in town. He practically owned everything, including a piece of the BDSM club where he and Ava met up. There would be no way he would be taking her back there any time soon.

"We don't even know that my father was behind the break- in," she said. Corbin looked at her as if she had to be crazy. Sure, they didn't have concrete proof, but what other explanation was there for a strange man showing up at their home the same night she told her father that she had beat him at his own game and gotten married. "Well, it's true," she said, defensively. "What if it was just some guy looking for a payday and he just so happens to break into your penthouse?"

Corbin rolled his eyes, "It's our penthouse and that might be a plausible explanation if something had been taken, but nothing was. Hell, he could have had quite a payday with everything I had just laying around but he took nothing. It just doesn't add up."

"When will we know more?" Ava asked. He had been waiting to tell her this next part. Corbin didn't want to get her hopes up and honestly, he was hoping to sneak down to his office in the lobby while she was working. He had promised to keep her in the loop, but until he had firsthand information to give her, he wanted to try to handle things himself.

"In about an hour," he admitted. "Rob called to tell me he had a clean picture from the video footage and he was bringing it over personally." He could feel her heated stare and Corbin knew that keeping that bit of information to himself was a shitty idea.

"And you were going to tell me this when?" she questioned.

"After the meeting," he admitted. Corbin knew better than to lie to Ava—she'd have his balls and he had grown rather fond of them.

She growled and stood from the sofa, all but throwing her laptop down onto the coffee table. "Corbin James Eklund," she shouted. He winced at the use of his middle name. His mother was the only other person in his life that ever middle named him and he had to admit, when Ava said it, it didn't seem to have the same effect as when his mom did. Honestly, it made him kind of hot, but he knew to keep that part to himself—at least for now.

He stood and crossed the room, standing over her body, loving the way his fierce wife didn't even stammer. Backing down wasn't her thing and he loved how she stood up not just for her friends, but also for herself. "Ava," he whispered.

"Don't you Ava me," she yelled, pressing her little finger into his chest. God, everything she was doing was having the opposite effect on him of what she was probably hoping for. He found the whole scene hot and he wondered just how she'd feel about him stripping her bare and sinking into her body.

"Is this our first official fight?" he whispered. Ava leaned into his body and he had his answer—she was just as hot and bothered by him as he was her.

"Don't try to distract me," she insisted, pressing both of her palms into his bare chest. Ava was wearing just his dress shirt and he knew from watching her get dressed earlier, that she had nothing on underneath it. They had spent most of the past two days completely naked and if he had his way, they'd be that way again in the next few minutes.

"Am I?" he taunted.

"Are you what?" she whispered.

"Distracting you?" he asked.

"Yes," she said, her lips so close to his he could almost feel them brush against his own.

A sharp knock at the door had Ava almost jumping into his arms. "Fuck," he swore. "Hold that thought, baby," he ordered. Corbin crossed the hotel suite and pulled the door open, ready to murder whoever had interrupted them.

"This better be good," he growled. His head of security stood on the other side of the door and looked Corbin up and down and smirked. Rob nodded and strode past him into the room as if Corbin wasn't a threat to him. It was one of the things he liked best about the guy—nothing seemed to faze him, not even a man Corbin's size with an even bigger attitude problem.

"Sorry to interrupt, Mrs. Eklund," Rob said. Corbin suddenly realized what his wife was wearing and growled his frustration.

"For the love of fuck, Rob," Corbin shouted." At least turn around until my wife can put some clothes on," Rob turned to face him, giving Ava some privacy, and had the nerve to smile at him, as if he enjoyed the whole song and dance they had going on between them. Ava giggled and pulled a blanket from the back of the sofa and wrapped it around her body.

"All clear," she said.

"Sorry, Mrs. Eklund," Rob said but Corbin knew he didn't mean a damn word of his apology.

"It's not a big deal, Rob. My husband is just a bit on edge. You have news?" Ava asked, as if taking charge of their little meeting. Rob nodded and sat down on the sofa, waiting for the two of them to join him.

"I do and I'm not sure you're going to like it, Mrs. Eklund," he said. Corbin sat down in an armchair and pulled Ava onto his lap. If it was news she wasn't going to like, he was going to damn well be there for her to help her through it.

"Alright," she stuttered. Corbin was sure he could feel her heart beating and he hated that they were going to have to face the possibility that whoever was in their penthouse was there to hurt his wife. "Just say it," she ordered. "I'm ready."

Rob took a deep breath and let it out. "It's your brother," he said. "Ashton Michaels."

Ava gasped, "No—it can't be," she said. "We haven't heard from him in over twenty years. He disappeared and my family believed him dead." Ava reached a shaking hand to her mouth, to muffle her sob, and it nearly broke Corbin's heart.

"What's he fucking want?" Corbin questioned.

"I'm not really sure yet," Rob admitted. "But, as soon as I have any more information, I'll be in touch." He stood and handed Corbin an envelope which he assumed had Ava's brother's picture in it.

"Thanks, Rob," he said, giving a curt nod. Rob turned and left the suite, pulling the door shut behind him and Ava's soft sobs filled the room. Corbin felt helpless in knowing what to do for her, but he knew one thing— there would be no fucking way that her brother or anyone else in her damn family was ever going to get close enough to hurt his wife again.

AVALON

"Pack your fucking bags," Corbin growled. "We're going to France."

"But, I thought you just said we weren't going," Ava said. "We can't run from this mess, Corbin. If Ashton is alive and he was the guy in our apartment, I need to find out why. Let me talk to him." She could tell by the expression on his face that Corbin wasn't going to agree to her request before he even opened his mouth.

"No," he said. Corbin crossed his arms over his massive chest and she knew that he had already made up his mind. "Getting you out of town is the best option."

"But you said," she tried arguing, but he covered her mouth with his big hand.

"I know what I said, honey. I also know that until we know for sure why your brother is back and was in our home; I can't take any chances with you. I'll call to have my jet fueled and ready to leave within the hour. Pack your stuff but don't tell your partner we are leaving yet.

You can call him when we get there and fill him in. I don't want any loose ends." Corbin waited her out as if he expected her to give him an argument.

Ava nodded and pulled his hand from her mouth. "Fine," she agreed. "But for the record, I think that running and hiding is an awful idea. I don't know why Ash was in our home but he's still my brother. I don't believe he was there to hurt me. The sooner we get answers the sooner we can put this mess behind us."

"It's too much of a coincidence, Ava. He showed up the same night we announce to your father that we're married. What if the two of them are working together? Do you trust your father?" Corbin asked. He already knew her answer and Ava hated that he was playing that card.

"No," she said. "You know I don't trust him and with good reason. But, that doesn't mean that Ash is bad too. It could just be a coincidence." Corbin shot her a disbelieving look and she sighed, knowing she had lost the fight. Really, she shouldn't be too upset—she was getting what she originally wanted, to go to France. That was before she found out that Ashton was the man in their penthouse. It was before she found out that her long lost brother was back from the dead. Going to France was the last thing she wanted to do now. But, convincing her husband not to run wasn't an option he seemed willing to explore.

Corbin rushed Ava through packing and ushered her

down to the lobby, surrounded by his security team. She was sure that even an armored tank wouldn't be able to reach her through the army he had amassed to keep her safe.

"Is this all really necessary?" Ava asked.

"You are mine and I will protect you how I want to, Ava," Corbin growled. He stayed close to her side and she had to admit that Corbin having her back through all this mess gave her comfort. Just knowing that he meant every one of his promises made her feel safer.

"I appreciate that, I really do, Corbin. But, I think this is all a little overkill. If Ashton is the one who is after me, he won't hurt me. I'm his sister." She knew she had no real proof that her brother wouldn't hurt her. Hell, her own father wanted to hurt her for just marrying the man she had fallen in love with. Of course, her dad didn't know that part. As far as her father was concerned, she had married Corbin out of spite, to keep her grandfather's money. Could that be the reason Ash had come back? She didn't want to believe the worst of him but she really had no other information to go on.

Corbin helped her into the waiting SUV and slid in next to her. As soon as they were both in the car, it pulled off from the curb and Corbin had slung his arm protectively around her shoulder. "Tell me about your brother, honey," he ordered. Since finding out that Ashton was the one in their home, she had been racking her brain trying to remember every detail of her older brother. Sadly, he left when she was still so young that she had forgotten a good deal about him.

"He disappeared when I was about nine. He had

gone away to college and even pledged a fraternity. He seemed happy every time he came home on break, and I honestly hated him for it. Our mother died about four years prior and I was miserable being left at home with my father and nannies," she said.

"Yes, you told me about how your father liked to work his way through your nannies. That must have been hard—not having any real stability at home," Corbin offered.

"Yeah, I had my Grandpa and I got to go over to his house on weekends, but my father wasn't around a whole lot. He split his time between Washington, D.C. and here. I was lonely, besides the time that I spent with my grandfather. I learned early on not to get attached to my nannies and self-reliance became my refuge," Ava admitted. It wasn't until Ava got to college and met Zara that she started to come out of her shell. Zara saved her in more ways than one and she knew her best friend felt the same. They became each other's family and Ava even considered Zara her sister.

"Zara was the person who eventually helped to pull me from my shell. I guess that's why I'm so fierce when it comes to anyone or anything trying to hurt her. That's why I gave Aiden such a hard time when we all first met." Corbin laughed.

"You were pretty fantastic at giving Aiden crap, honey," he said. Corbin kissed her cheek and she smiled up at him. "Tell me more about Ashton," he prompted.

She thought back to the time after her brother seemed to disappear from the face of the earth and frowned. "The night we got news that he disappeared was so chaotic. I was at home alone with the nanny of the month and we were woken in the middle of the night by the cops banging at our front door. She tried to tell me to go back to sleep—that everything would be alright, but she was wrong. I went back upstairs, but hid at the end of the hallway, out of sight, to eavesdrop. I heard the cops ask where my brother was and she told them that he should be in his dormitory at school. They kept asking questions," Ava remembered.

"What kind of questions?" Corbin asked.

"Um—stuff like what kind of car he drove and if he had a girlfriend or boyfriend. The nanny kept telling them she had no idea and the cop accused her of being uncooperative. They threatened to take her down to the station to answer questions if she refused to cooperate. That's about the time that my grandfather showed up. He told my nanny to go back to her room and called me down from my hiding spot in the hallway."

Corbin chuckled, "He knew you were there, listening?"

"Yep," she said. "He knew me inside and out. I couldn't get away with anything when he was around." Ava giggled at the memory. He always knew what she was up to and usually called her on her shit. If it wasn't for him, Ava would have been allowed to get away with just about anything and there was no telling the person she would have turned out to be.

"I think I would have liked your Grandpa, Ava," Corbin admitted.

"I know he would have liked you, Corbin," she said. She had thought about that a few times since meeting

Corbin, whether her Grandpa would have approved of her marrying a man like Corbin Eklund. He was never so stuffy to buy into that new and old money business that her father had. Ava was sure that her grandfather would have wholeheartedly approved of her choice of Corbin and that thought made her happy.

"Did you get into trouble?" he asked.

"Nope." She smiled at him triumphantly and Corbin chuckled, shaking his head at her. "He told me that it wasn't polite to spy on people and to go to my room. I didn't dare disobey him and try to listen in on the rest of the conversation." Ava shivered against Corbin. Her grandfather was a fair man, but if crossed he wasn't pleasant to deal with.

"Was that when you found out Ashton was missing?" Corbin asked.

"No, not that night. I woke up the next morning full of questions, but my Grandpa was gone. The nanny pretended that nothing had happened the night before. She even had the nerve to brush off my questions about the cops showing up at my house as me having bad dreams. But, I knew what I saw," she said.

"Shit," Corbin swore. "What did you do?"

"I waited until that next weekend. I knew the only person who would give me an honest answer would be my grandfather. I pretended to forget all about the cop's visit but as soon as I got to my Grandpa's house, it was as if everything I was holding in that whole week exploded out of me." Corbin laughed again. "Yeah, that was the same reaction my grandfather had too," Ava admitted.

"I bet. You do have a way with words, baby," he teased. Ava slapped at his chest and giggled.

"Well, it didn't do me any good. He told me nothing except that Ashton was missing. They didn't know where he was or when he'd be back." Ava felt the same sadness she had when her Grandpa told her about her brother all over again. She remembered how upset he seemed when he told her and if she wasn't mistaken, he even shed a tear as he told her about Ash.

"I'm sorry, honey," Corbin said, cuddling her into his side. "But, why did you believe he was dead?"

"After a few years, I just assumed it to be true. My father didn't allow any talk of Ashton in our home. It was the same way when my mother died—we weren't allowed to even bring up her name." Ava remembered wanting to talk to anyone who'd listen about her mother, but that wasn't allowed. Her father even went so far as to forbid her nannies to talk to her about her mom. It was a very confusing time for her.

"I wanted to remember them both, but it wasn't allowed," she admitted.

"You were just a little girl, honey. Of course you just wanted to talk about your mom and brother," Corbin soothed. Ava thought her father was just upset about losing them both, but after time she came to realize that it was a form of control for him. He started to control everything about her—from what she said and thought to who she hung out with. It was one of the main reasons she had no real friends in high school. She shut herself off from the world and that girl was someone she never wanted to be again.

"Somewhere along the way, I just started believing that Ashton was dead like my mother. No one corrected me and that was that. Now—" Her voice cracked and Ava hated feeling so helpless. Corbin wrapped his arms around her tighter.

"Now," he said. "We find out just where the hell your brother has been all this time and figure out why he was in our home. You have me now, honey and I'll be by your side the whole time and we'll figure it out together." Ava nodded, not sure she could speak passed the lump of emotion in her throat.

"Thank you, Corbin," she whispered.

"No need to ever thank me, honey. You're my wife and we do all of this together from now on."

"Deal," she said, smiling up at him. Corbin gently kissed her lips and Ava wondered just what she had done to deserve such a man in her life. She wasn't going to question it though because he was hers now and there wasn't anything she'd want to do to change that.

Corbin gave instructions to his pilot and Ava hated that they were going to France. Sure, she had all but begged him to take her there just that morning, but now it felt more like they were running away from their problems. She wanted to start facing down her demons and going to France now felt wrong; not that there would be any way for her to change her husband's mind on the matter. He had seemed to make his decision just as soon as his head of security showed up at the hotel with news about Ashton.

He ushered her onto the waiting jet that his and Aiden's company owned and went to find the pilot. Ava sent Zara a quick text telling her that she was fine but they had a change in plans. Hell, her entire life was starting to feel like one giant change of plans and she wondered if or when that would ever be different.

Corbin made quite a ruckus entering the plane and she didn't bother to look up from her phone. She needed a few minutes to get herself together and if pretending to talk to Zara bought her time, she'd use it to her advantage.

"Avalon." Ava heard his voice and knew exactly who was talking to her, but she worried that when she looked up, she wouldn't find her brother standing in front of her. She tightly closed her eyes, like when she was a child and wanted to hide from whoever was trying to talk to her. Ava always foolishly believed that if she couldn't see someone, they wouldn't be able to see her.

"Ava, please look at me," Ash whispered.

"No," she said. "You aren't here and this isn't real. You're supposed to be dead." Her brother barked out his laugh, causing her to jump in her seat. Ava opened her eyes and stood. There would be no hiding from the person who was now mere inches away from her. If her brother was there to do her harm, she'd find a way to get to Corbin.

"What the fuck?" Corbin growled from the door. "Ava, tell me you are alright," he ordered.

She nodded, "I'm fine, Corbin."

"Come here," he said. She didn't hesitate, brushing passed Ashton to stand by Corbin. He pulled her protectively against his side and she swore she could hear his heart beating.

"Ava, please," her brother begged. "Just talk to me."

"Ashton," Ava squeaked and cleared her throat. She wasn't going to let him know how much he had upset her. Ash owed her explanations and she was going to keep her wits about her and ask him for those answers. "How are you here?" Corbin tugged at her arm, as if he wanted to get her the hell out of there, but the way her brother was watching her, he looked just as upset about the whole situation as she felt. "I'm okay, Corbin," she lied. "This is my brother, Ashton. Or, at least I think he's my brother." Ava looked him up and down and honestly, she wasn't quite sure if the man standing in front of her was the same boy who had left them years ago. Ash looked so different now but she knew firsthand how time could change people.

"Hey Sis," he whispered. "It's been a while."

"That's what you say to me after not having any contact for over twenty years? God, Ash—I thought you were dead. How could you just leave with no word? Do you know what losing you did to Grandpa?"

"Please believe that if there was any other way, I would have done everything differently. But there wasn't," Ashton said.

"I'm sorry if I don't buy that you had no choice but to leave our family, and especially our grandfather, completely broken- hearted, Ash," Ava spat.

"Grandpa was the one who came up with the idea for me to leave," Ashton admitted. Ava belted out her laugh and shook her head, as if she was trying to shake the image of her beloved grandfather forcing her brother to leave town.

"You said you had no other choice," Corbin interrupted. "Mind telling us what you mean by that?" Ava shot him a look as if he had lost his mind and he just shrugged it off.

Ash nodded, "I did something that would have ruined our family and I was sent away. Honestly, it was the best decision for everyone."

Avalon bravely took a step towards Ash. "It wasn't the best decision for me, Ash," Ava shouted. "You left me with a monster and after Grandpa died, I had no one."

"I know, Sis and if I could take back any of your pain and suffering, I would." Ashton reached for her and she took a step away from him, backing right into Corbin's body. He wrapped his arms around her and she had to admit, she was thankful for his support.

"Why did you break into our home?" Corbin growled.

"To warn you, Ava," Ashton said, looking directly at her. "Dad will stop at nothing to keep you from getting all of Grandpa's money. He's lost everything and you were his last hope of holding onto the family fortune."

"Tell me why Grandpa would send you away like that, Ash," she demanded. "Make me understand why you left." She sounded like she was begging him and hell, maybe she was, but Ava didn't care.

"It's a long story," he said.

169

"We've got time," Corbin said. "And, if you think about trying to leave, you should know that I have two armed guards waiting just outside the plane to take you into custody."

"I don't want any trouble," Ashton admitted. "I just want to warn my sister—keep her safe."

"Then we are in agreement because I will do whatever it takes to keep my wife safe," Corbin said.

Ash smiled, "I like him." He crossed the fuselage to the jet's mini bar and pulled a bottle of scotch down, pouring himself a generous portion. He swallowed it back in one and turned to face Avalon. "Sorry," he said. "I needed a little liquid courage. This isn't going to be pretty and you aren't going to like any of it, Ava," he admitted.

"If you can't tell," Ava said, holding her arms wide, "I'm all grown up now."

"I see that and you turned out good, baby sister," Ash said, smiling over at her. Ava could see the sadness behind his eyes and worried that he was right about one thing, she wasn't going to like what he was about to tell her.

"Just tell me, Ash," she begged.

He sat down in one of the leather seats, leaning back into the plush cushions. "My freshman year in college, I killed someone," he said. Avalon gasped, covering her mouth with her hands.

"Fuck," Corbin swore. Ava shot him a sideways glance and he held up his hands, as if telling her he'd back down and let her handle things with her brother. Ava knew that

Corbin wouldn't let her have the floor for long. He liked his control, but he also seemed to know that she needed to get to the bottom of what was going on with Ashton.

"How?" she asked.

"Hit and run," Ashton said. "I went to one of those stupid fraternity parties and I was a fool. I was pledging the fraternity and got way too drunk; apparently that didn't stop me from getting behind the wheel and trying to drive home. I hit a woman who was walking home from a bus stop and killed her, instantly. I woke up in our driveway. Apparently, I blacked out and don't remember the accident, which is my only saving grace. When I realized what I had done, I was a coward and I ran—straight to Grandpa and he told me he'd fix everything."

"You didn't go to the police?" Corbin questioned.

"No," Ash whispered. "It would have ended both Dad and Grandpa's careers. They wouldn't allow it. I begged Grandpa to let me turn myself in. Days after the accident, I felt so much guilt I wanted to do the right thing but he refused. He didn't tell Dad at first and by the time it was all over, I was picking up with a new life across the country and no one was the wiser. You were just a kid, but I have to admit leaving you was the hardest part."

"You left without a word," she cried and Corbin tightened his arms around her.

"I said goodbye to you, Sis. You were sleeping at the time," Ashton said. "The night I left, I snuck into your room and kissed your forehead and told you how sorry

I was. It was just before the police showed up at the door and Grandpa shooed them away."

"You were there that night?" Ava asked. "Why didn't you say something?"

"I couldn't. He made me promise that I'd do exactly as he wanted. Hell, he didn't even know I showed up at the house until the next day. I just couldn't leave without seeing you one last time. So, I snuck out of Grandpa's house and by the time I got to Dad's, you were sound asleep. I hid in your closet when the police showed up and woke you and your nanny up. I snuck out the back of the house when Grandpa caught you eavesdropping and didn't look back. The next day, he told me that he knew that I had left his house and gone to see you. He was furious that I disobeyed him and I was so worried that he might change his mind about helping me, I panicked," Ash admitted. "I promised to do whatever he wanted and he sent me away."

"Why come back now?" Corbin asked. "You obviously got away with it, so why risk coming back now?"

"Because Dad is completely off his rocker and if you're not careful, he'll use whatever means necessary to keep you from getting your hands on Grandpa's money. Dad must have found out about what I did and how Grandpa helped me. That was how he got his old man to put the marriage stipulation into his will. He basically blackmailed him to add that fucking clause, never expecting you to settle down."

"Well, that explains everything. I wondered how Dad got Grandpa to agree to that crazy clause. He would have never willingly handed over control to Dad unless he had no choice," Avalon said.

"You're right. They hated each other and I'm betting Dad pulled out all the stops when he stuck it to Grandpa," Ash said.

"How is your father out of money?" Corbin asked. That was a good question. Even without her grandfather's fortune, her father would have inherited enough money, to keep him in the lifestyle he was accustomed to, from his mother. Both of her grandparents came from well-to-do families and old money. That was part of the reason why her Grandpa didn't want her dad getting his hands on his money. Her grandmother had doted on her father and made sure that he'd never want for anything. Maybe that was the reason her father and grandfather never really got along. Ava didn't personally know her grandmother, but from what she had gathered, she wasn't a very nice person.

"You know Dad has a problem with keeping his pants zipped up. He made a few bad decisions in his personal life and with the few businesses that he bought into. He's broke, Ava," Ashton said. "Grandpa's money is his last hope and you're the only thing standing between him and that fortune."

"Correction," Corbin barked. "We're the only thing standing between your father and Ava's money. If I have a say in all of this, and I do now that Ava is my wife, your dad won't touch a penny of it."

Ashton smiled again, reminding Ava of the young boy she used to know. "Yep, I like him."

"So, now what?" Ava asked. "You just disappear into

the shadows again and I'm supposed to pretend that you're dead?

"No," Ash breathed. "I'm turning myself in. It's the right thing to do. It's time I paid for my crimes and made things right. Besides, Grandpa's gone and I don't give a fuck about Dad's non-existent political career."

Ava hated thinking about her brother being locked away but he was right. He committed a crime and their family had kept his secret for long enough. "You said you have guards outside?" Ash asked Corbin. Her husband reluctantly nodded. "Good, tell them that I'm in here and I wish to surrender." Corbin looked down at Ava and she nodded.

"He's right," she said. "It's for the best."

"I'll be right back," he promised, turning to leave the plane.

"Will you come visit me?" Ash almost whispered his question.

"Of course," she promised. "Whenever I can." Ava crossed the plane's small cabin and wrapped her arms around her brother. "You're my brother, Ash and I love you."

"Love you too, squirt," he choked. Corbin walked back onto the jet with his two security guards and Ava watched as they took her brother into custody. She was proud of herself for keeping it together until they removed him from the plane and then she broke down in Corbin's arms. She allowed herself to fall apart knowing that he'd be there to catch her.

CORBIN

Corbin listened to his wife's sobs and they nearly broke his heart. It was almost too much but he knew she needed him now more than ever. "We're going to be okay, honey," he soothed.

"I know but it just doesn't feel that way at the moment," she admitted. "We can't go to France right now, Corbin. I need to be here for Ashton. He'll need a lawyer and someone in his corner." He hated the idea of sticking around and giving her father a chance to make good on his threats. Her dad had hired a team of lawyers to poke into their marriage and try to prove that they had married for her inheritance. He worried that the truth would come out and he hated that Ava might lose everything. They might have started out getting hitched as a way for her to keep her grandfather's money, but it had turned into so much more. He was completely in love with her and he knew she felt the same way about him.

The fact remained that she had married him as a

way to keep her money and if her father's lawyers could prove that fact in a court of law, she'd lose everything she was fighting so hard to keep. "But your father," he protested.

"Can go straight to hell. I'm done running and hiding from him. If he wants to come at me, let him. What he's going to find is a woman who's willing and ready to fight for what she wants now," Ava said.

"And a man who's completely in love with her, who's also willing to fight alongside of her." Ava turned to face him and smiled.

"I love you too, Corbin. Let's fight this—together," she said, holding out her hand, waiting for him to take her up on her offer. Corbin didn't feel even the slightest hesitancy, reaching for her hand and taking it in his own.

"Together," he agreed.

"So, what do we do first?" Ava asked and he laughed. God, he loved his woman.

"First, we go home and take our lives back. No more running and no more hiding. Then, I think we need to use our resources and get some people in high places involved. I think that once your father sees that he can't bully his way out of this, he might back down." Ava shot him a look that told him she didn't believe him, but she would.

"We have friends in high places?" she asked.

"Sure—I happen to even know a Senator," Corbin teased. "It's time to come clean with our friends and tell Aiden and Zara what's really been going on between us. They'll understand."

"I doubt that Zara will be so understanding, but you're right. It's time to stop going it alone. I've done that for so long, I've forgotten what it's like to have someone in my life that has my back."

"Baby, I'll always have your back—and your front," Corbin teased, bobbing his eyebrows at her to drive his point home. Ava's giggle filled the jet's cabin and for the first time in days, Corbin felt as if everything might be alright.

"Let's go home," Ava said and he had to admit, that sounded like one hell of a plan.

"You want to say that again?" Zara shouted. She handed her daughter to Aiden as she rounded the sofa to confront Corbin and he had to admit, he was scared of what she planned on doing next. Not too many women scared the shit out of him, but Zara was one of them.

"He married me to help me keep my money," Ava said. They had already been through all this a couple times, but Zara refused to just accept what they were telling her.

"You just settled?" Zara growled at Ava. Corbin tried to tuck her behind his body but Ava wouldn't have it. She stepped out from behind him and faced her friend head on.

"I did not settle," Ava spat. "I love Corbin and he loves me. It just started out as a way for me to keep my grandfather's money, but it turned into more."

Zara pointed her finger into Corbin's chest and he

knew she was far from finished giving him the run around. "You did this," she accused. "You fed on my best friend's moment of weakness; saw your in with her and took it." She poked her boney little finger into his chest with just about every word, as if accenting her point.

"No, he didn't," Ava defended, stepping between him and Zara's offensive finger. "I was the one who took advantage of him. I wanted him to marry me and he said yes."

"How about I put Lexi in her crib and the four of us sit down like adults to discuss this?" Aiden asked. "The girls will be home soon and I don't want them to see us fighting."

"You're right," Zara agreed. "Then Corbin can explain to us how he plans on making this all right with Ava. You can't just use her and dump her."

"Woah," Corbin protested. "Now that's going too far, Zara. You can yell at me and berate me all you'd like but don't ever accuse me of using Ava. I'd never do that and there is no fucking way I'm going to ever dump her." The idea of losing Ava scared the crap out of him and he wouldn't let Zara imply that was even a possibility.

"Zara, honey, let's just hear them out before we start accusing anyone of anything," Aiden insisted. Corbin nodded his thanks and his friend disappeared upstairs with the baby.

"How about you help me with some food, Ava," Zara insisted. Ava looked back at him as her best friend pulled her into the kitchen and he smiled and shrugged. Corbin needed a reprieve and maybe that made him a complete fucking chicken, but he didn't give a shit.

Aiden came jogging back down the stairs and peeked into the kitchen to where the two girls were talking, probably about him. "Geeze man, why would you go and open up a whole can of worms like that? You had to know that Zara would react to your news that way. What were you thinking?"

"That I need your help," Corbin admitted. He hadn't gotten to that part. Zara hadn't given him or Ava the chance to get to the part where they believed that her father would stop at nothing to get his hands on her money.

"My help?" Aiden asked. "You know you never even have to ask for that. Whatever you need, I'm here for you, man." Corbin breathed a sigh of relief. He knew that Aiden was true to his word and that he could always count on his best friend to have his back, but hearing him say the words felt as if a burden had been lifted off Corbin's chest.

"Thanks for that, Aiden," he said. "I think Ava's in trouble."

"In trouble how?" Aiden asked.

"I think that her father realizes that he's about to lose at this little game he has been playing and he's flat broke. He won't let her walk away with her grandfather's money and I won't let him anywhere near my wife," Corbin admitted.

"Okay, let's get the women back in here and we can talk this through. I think you should start at the beginning and we'll figure things out from there," Aiden promised. As if on cue, Zara and Ava returned with their arms full of food and it was as if things weren't vamped up and heated between them just moments before. But, that was the way things were with them. It was the way things worked in a family and Corbin was damn happy that he had both Aiden and Zara behind them. They needed all the help they could get at this point.

"First, we eat," Zara insisted, setting the plates down on the table. "Then, we plot. There is no way Ava's father is going to touch one cent of her grandfather's money," she said. "Not if I have anything to say about it."

AVALON

"I'm going to take a quick shower and then I will come back and we can veg out and watch some television, if you'd like," Corbin offered. He had been so quiet the whole car ride home from Zara and Aiden's, she was starting to worry that she had done something wrong. What she really wanted from her husband was the chance to show him how much she needed his dominance. It had been days since Corbin had commanded her body, mind and soul and it was about time she reminded him how well they worked together.

Ava slyly nodded and watched as he walked back to their master bathroom. As soon as she heard the water turn on, she tugged her clothes off and stood naked in the middle of their bedroom. The urge to touch herself made her half-crazy with lust. She knew it was one of Corbin's hard and fast BDSM rules—he liked to control all her orgasms, but she was already topping from the bottom and she was pretty sure that act alone was going to earn her a few spankings.

Ava snaked her hand down her body and found her already wet, throbbing clit and hesitantly ran her fingers over it. She moaned at just how good that felt. She sunk to her knees and palmed her breasts, needing more. Ava worked two of her fingers in and out of her pussy, wishing they were her husband's cock, needing more pleasure than she could ever give herself. She had just about found her release when Corbin emerged still wet from the shower, to find her kneeling on their bedroom floor, masturbating.

"Well, I see someone has thrown all of my rules right out the window," he growled. She looked up at him through her lust fueled haze and wondered if she was going to be punished before or after she found her release. Her husband was quite ruthless when it came to withholding her orgasms when she broke his rules.

"Corbin, please," she whimpered, not bothering to remove her fingers from her drenched folds. "I need you so much."

He barked out his laugh, dropping his towel to show off his already impressive erection. "Looks like you're doing pretty good there all by yourself, sweetheart." He stroked his heavy shaft through his hands and threw back his head, his sexy lips parted on a moan.

"Fuck," Ava swore. "That's so fucking hot, Corbin. Please can I taste you?" she begged.

"Sure, baby," he said, staring her down. "Just as soon as you tell me what this little show is all about."

Ava pouted and he chuckled, not letting go of his cock. She couldn't take her eyes off him and she worried that he was going to leave her wet and needy in the middle of their bedroom floor while he found his release. He was stubborn enough to wait her out and knowing that left her no choice but to admit to her feelings.

"Fine," she said, sitting back on her heels, gifting him with the perfect view of her pussy. "I miss you."

"So you said," he teased. "But what you're doing has nothing to do with me. In fact, it's breaking one of my rules," he said.

"Two actually," she whispered, inwardly cursing herself for saying anything that would get her in deeper trouble.

"Sorry?" Aiden questioned. "You broke two rules?" he asked.

"Yeah, although it's technically not a rule. I'm topping from the bottom," she said.

"Hmm," he hummed and just that little sound had a fresh wave of wetness coating her thighs. "Looks like you're right," he said. "So, I take it this is your way of telling me you don't want to watch a movie cuddled up in bed tonight?" he teased.

"No," Ava breathed. "I need you, Corbin—all of you. Ever since this thing with the break-in happened and the whole mess with Ash, you haven't touched me."

"That's not exactly true," he defended. "We've made love since finding out about your brother." He wasn't wrong. They had sex a few times a day but he was always so careful not to push her. She could tell he was holding back with her and Ava hated that.

"I need all of you, Corbin," she said. Ava fought to hold back her tears. She needed to get through this without crying. Corbin seemed to pick up on her distress and crossed the room to stand in front of her.

"Tell me what's going on, Ava," he ordered.

"I can tell that you're holding back from me. You aren't giving me your full dominance and I need that from you right now, Corbin. Especially now," she sobbed.

Corbin grabbed handfuls of her hair and gave a sharp yank, getting her attention. "Open," he ordered. "You want my dominance and I'll give it to you, baby. When we are done here, I'll be giving you your punishment and I'm pretty sure you won't be able to sit down on that sexy, curvy ass of yours for days." Ava's body hummed to life with his promise and she willingly opened her mouth, letting him slide his cock all the way in to the back of her throat. Ava loved the way Corbin took control, pumping himself in and out of her mouth.

"Touch yourself," he ordered. "Finish being naughty for me, honey." Ava looked up his body to find him watching her and she knew better than to disobey him again. She reached back down and let her fingers glide through her slick pussy and moaned around his cock. "God, Ava," he growled. "I'm not going to last much longer if you keep doing shit like that. I want you with me. Get yourself off," he ordered.

She bucked and writhed on her fingers as they slid in and out of her wet folds. When Corbin reached down to pinch her taut nipple between his thumb and finger, she couldn't take anymore. She felt as though she was flying and when Corbin threw his head back and moaned her name, she knew he was just about ready to lose himself down her throat. He pumped in and out of her mouth a few more times, until he shot his seed into her willing mouth. Ava took everything he was giving her and licked his cock clean.

"Good girl," he hoarsely praised. "Now, for your punishment," he taunted.

Ava smiled up at him, not hiding how much she was looking forward to everything his sinful voice promised. "Yes, Sir," she enthusiastically said. Corbin chuckled and ran his hand down her jaw to cup her chin.

"Don't play games with me," he said. "If you want or need something from me, all you have to do is tell me, Ava. I'm sorry I've been holding back with you lately. You were right—I was worried about how you were holding up with everything that was happening and I should have known my tough girl would be able to take just about anything life threw her way." Ava soaked up his praise, not quite sure how she had gotten so lucky in the husband department but she wasn't about to start questioning things now. Corbin was hers and that was all that mattered.

"Now, up on the bed and show me that ass," he ordered. "I'm going to spank it red and then fuck you from behind, Wife," he said.

"Yes sir," she agreed because what else could she do? Her Dom gave her a command and Ava was nothing but obedient.

"You will keep count for me, Ava," he ordered. "This isn't for your pleasure and I won't go easy on you." She felt almost giddy with anticipation at Corbin's promise.

This was exactly what she had been craving. He was everything she needed and so much more—she just needed all of him, no holding back.

"Yes, sir," she said. She crawled onto the bed and laid face down on the soft comforter, her knees bent under her and her ass up in the air for Corbin, just as he demanded. He groaned and ran his big hand down her bare ass, cupping her sex.

"This is mine after we are finished with your punishment, Avalon," he said.

"Yes, sir," she stuttered. "Everything I have is yours." She meant it too; Corbin owned every inch of her, including her heart.

"Count," he growled. Corbin landed the first blow on her left cheek and she whimpered from the after sting that seemed to burn her skin. Honestly, it took her breath away and she was having trouble being able to count out loud. "Ava," he warned.

"One," she sobbed.

"Baby, if this is too much, you know your safe word," he soothed. She knew her safe word alright but she was determined not to use it. This was what she had asked him for and he was finally giving her all of himself. She could handle all of Corbin—there would be no backing down from his challenge.

"I'm fine," Sir," she said.

"We'll go to ten," he said, landing the second blow on her right cheek.

"Two," she said, gritting her teeth to get through the sting of pain. Corbin set a punishing rhythm, not giving Ava much time to recover between blows. By the time he got to ten, she was sobbing, tears rolling down her face and she was sure her ass was marked with red welts.

"Ten," she whispered.

"Tell me you're okay," Corbin said. Ava could hear the raw emotion in his voice and she wanted to reassure him that she was fine. She kneeled in front of him and put her arms around his neck.

"I am," she said. "This is us, Corbin. You are what I need and not giving this to me—holding yourself back from me—it hurts."

"I promise that won't happen again, honey," he said. "I just got so caught up with keeping you safe and making sure that you were emotionally coping with all of the shit being thrown at you, that I forgot what you needed from me."

"Well, I didn't really mind having to remind you," she teased.

"That was quite a display you put on for me, baby. You sure do know how to get my attention," he said. "I promise to find a balance, for us both, but you have to know that keeping you safe in all of this will be my top priority."

"I understand," she said. "I just need for things to go back to normal, Corbin. Not just between the two of us but in our everyday lives. We weren't away for that long, but I have work piling up for me at the office. My partner can only take so many more days of me calling in to tell him that I won't be able to make it in again. I need normal." Corbin was quiet and she knew that he was mentally trying to figure out her request. She was quickly learning that her husband always had a plan and right now, he seemed to be executing their new "normal" lives in his mind.

Ava giggled, "I think you might be overthinking things more than I usually do, if that's even possible," she teased.

"I'm trying to figure out just how 'normal' we can be when your father is still a threat. We got another package of questionnaires from his lawyers today at work. That makes three big envelopes of questions they are legally allowed to ask us about our marriage because of that damn stipulation your grandfather put in his will. Is it all really worth it, Ava?"

"Are you asking if it's worth all the trouble we're being put through, to keep my grandfather's money from my dad? Because, my answer will always be yes. If my father needs that money, like Ash said he does, then my answer is hell yes!" The thought of her father blowing through the money he got from his mother and then going after Ava's inheritance infuriated her. He was a greedy, selfish bastard and she would answer every question thrown at them if that's what it took to keep her father from her grandfather's money.

"Are the questions very personal?" she asked. Ava had a feeling that she already knew the answer and judging by the angry expression her sexy husband wore, she was correct.

"They want to know about our sex life," he grumbled.

"No," she breathed. "That's not any of my father's or anyone else's business. We just need to find a way to answer their questions without getting into specifics." Ava knew that would be easier said than done. Her father was going to try to break them down, to prove that their marriage was a sham. The problem for her dear old dad was that her marriage was as real as they came and there would be no way for him to prove otherwise. Not now, at least.

"Alright," he agreed. "We will need to sit down with our lawyers soon then and come up with answers that don't give all the personal details of our relationship away. I won't allow that, Ava. This," he said, motioning between their two bodies. "This is just between the two of us and is no one else's business."

"Agreed," she said. "Now, please make me yours," she begged.

"Deal," Corbin said, rolling her under his big body.

CORBIN

Corbin headed into the office for the first time in weeks and he wasn't sure that leaving Avalon was his best decision. The night before, he made Ava a promise that he would let life go back to normal and that meant they would both go back to their jobs. He loved that Aiden was willing to hold down the fort at work, but his wife was right, it was time for them to resume their regular schedules.

"Corbin," Rose said, meeting him at the private elevator that he and Aiden used, before he could even step free from the closing doors. She threw herself against him and wrapped her arms around his neck.

"Easy, Ma," he chided. "Let me get off the fucking elevator," he teased.

"Language, Corbin James," she chided. "I didn't raise you to be a caveman. I've missed you," she said.

"You just saw me a couple weeks ago, when Ava and I got back from France," he said.

"Yeah, but you haven't been around much and Aiden told me what was going on with Ava and her brother. I'm so sorry," Rose said. "How's she holding up?"

"She's tough," Corbin praised. He knew his girl would be able to get through whatever she'd have to in order to be by her brother's side in all this mess.

"Yes, she is," Rose agreed. He knew his mother liked his wife and he had to admit, he was thankful for that. It made his life so much easier knowing that the two women he loved most in the world, actually liked each other.

"Sorry that I wasn't the one to tell you about the crap going on with her family, Mom," Corbin said.

"No problem," Rose said. "As long as I'm kept in the loop, I don't care which one of my boys gives me the four-one-one," Corbin laughed at his mother's use of modern slang.

"Do not use that saying again, Ma," he begged.

"And why not? I'm young," she teased. "I've got it going on." Corbin groaned and started passed her, almost making it to his office when Aiden stopped him.

"She is, you know," Aiden agreed with Rose, feeding her ego. "Rose still has it going on, even if you refuse to see it, Corbin."

"Don't suck up to her. Lying to Mom only ends badly for both of us," Corbin said. Rose giggled and returned to her desk that sat between their two offices. Corbin liked knowing that his mom was so close. Most days, they had lunch together and he worried that sooner or later, she'd find a reason to leave them. She was always threatening to quit, but Corbin worried that if she did, he and Aiden would fall apart. She was their glue, but he'd never admit that to her.

"Can I talk to you for a minute?" Aiden asked. From the concern in his friend's eyes, he knew that it was something that couldn't wait. All the work that had piled up on his desk for the past two weeks would be there after they talked.

"Oh, Ma," he said, stopping at her desk on the way past, to Aiden's office. "Ava said to tell you that she wants you to come to dinner one night this week. Just call her and make the plans," he offered.

"That would be nice," Rose said.

Corbin joined Aiden in his office and turned to face him. "Okay, spill it. What has you looking like complete doom and gloom?" Corbin asked.

"I think you should sit down before I just spit it out," Aiden offered, nodding to the sofa that sat in front of his big desk.

"Fine." Corbin did as his friend asked, knowing that when Aiden got in one of his bossy moods, nothing would stop him from getting what he wanted. Corbin settled on the sofa and looked up at Aiden, expectantly.

"I talked to two of the fraternity brothers who were there the night of the party Ash attended." Corbin whistled at Aiden's news. "That was fast, man," he said. "You found them in less than a day."

"Well, they go to my club and when I was there this morning to work out, I ran into them. They told me that Ash was there and he was near blackout drunk, but he didn't drive home that night," Aiden said.

Corbin sat on the edge of the sofa. "What the hell?" he said.

Ash held up his hands, as if trying to rein Corbin's temper in. "Just hear me out, man and then your head can explode." He sat back, wanting to hear the rest but he felt about ready to jump out of his own damn skin.

"Sorry," he offered.

"No problem. Anyway," he continued, "they said that Ava's grandfather was never called. In fact, her father was the one who showed up to the house that night. He and Ash had a huge fight and he accused his son of trying to ruin their family. He demanded that Ashton leave with him and took his car keys from him. He was the one driving that night, not Ash."

"Fuck," Corbin swore.

"It gets better," Aiden said. "The guys were never questioned about that night. The officer in charge of the case never pursued the matter and it was just presumed that Ash was the one who was at fault, since he took off just after the accident."

"So, now what do we do?" Corbin asked. He wasn't sure what the next step was, but knowing Ava the way he did, she'd want Ashton out of that prison as soon as humanly possible. His only thought was how to keep his wife safe. If her father had gone to so much trouble to hide the truth all those years, Corbin was pretty sure he'd do much worse to keep them quiet.

"Let me do a little more digging. I'll use my resources to get to the bottom of this. Are you going to tell Ava?" Aiden asked.

Corbin barked out his laugh. There would never be a

secret he could keep from his wife. "Yeah, I'm pretty sure if she finds out that I kept a secret from her, she'd have my balls," Corbin said.

Aiden laughed, "Welcome to the club, man. We might think we're dominant but our wives keep our balls in their very expensive handbags." Corbin grimaced at the thought of Ava having him by the balls but in all honesty, he wouldn't want it any other way.

"My wife can do just about anything she wants to with my balls, man," Corbin teased. "But, I'm still going to tell her what you found out. She has a right to know." Aiden nodded. "Thanks for this, man," Corbin said. "I owe you one."

"You owe me a hell of a lot more than one, but we can call it even," Aiden teased. "You are my best friend," he said.

"Brother," Corbin corrected and walked out of his office.

Corbin spent the rest of the day worrying about having to tell Ava about Aiden's news. She wasn't going to be happy about the fact that her own father cared so little about his family that he all but destroyed both Ava and her brother. But, he wasn't a coward and he wouldn't hide from his own wife.

He had his driver drop him off at the front of the building. He rode his private elevator up to their penthouse and smiled at the sound of Ava singing off- key from their kitchen. His wife had taken to trying to cook for him and honestly, it was a toss-up as to which was worse—her singing or her cooking.

"Hey," he said, turning the corner to find her dancing around in her pajamas, singing into a spoon. "I see you got home early today," he said. Ava put down her spoon and crossed the kitchen to jump into his arms.

"Yep," she said. "It was an easy day in the office and I decided to knock of early and come home to make my husband dinner." Corbin eyed the half burnt concoction she was cooking up and laughed.

"Well, it's definitely your cooking, then," he said.

"What's my cooking?" Ava asked, seeming confused by his random remark.

"I was trying to decide which is worse, your singing or your cooking. That confirms it," he said pointing to the boiling pot. "Your cooking is."

"Well, it could have been good," she defended, eyeing the pot. "But, you came home early and ruined the surprise."

"Sure, honey," he teased. "Let's go with that. How about I help you clean up this mess and then we can order takeout?"

"Asian?" she questioned, causing Corbin to chuckle. His girl sure did love Asian takeout.

"Sure," he agreed. "I'm assuming you want your normal noodles with the sauce on the side and steamed vegetables?"

Ava enthusiastically nodded, "And, spring rolls and oh—that meat on a stick thing you get sometimes, get two of those for me. Also, don't forget the fortune cookies this time. In fact, order extra."

"Wow," he breathed. "You worked up an appetite today."

"I have been hungry all day and unfortunately—I've been eating all day, too. I guess I'm stress eating, but that's easier than punching everyone who annoys me or makes me mad." Corbin knew Ava had been going through a lot of crap with her brother's return. He hated that she was so stressed, but if Asian takeout helped, he'd do that and so much more for her.

"I have a few ideas of how we could work off some of your stress, honey," he said. Ava swatted at him and giggled.

"First food, then you can give me some stress management tips." Ava winked at him and turned to start to clean up the mess in the kitchen. Corbin placed the order for delivery and by the time he got back to the kitchen to help Ava, she was just about finished.

"Perfect timing," she teased. "You missed the whole gory mess."

"Well, I was hunting and foraging to bring home food for my woman," Corbin growled, giving her his best caveman imitation, even thumping his chest for good measure.

"My hero," she sassed, batting her eyelashes at him.

"Let's just hope you feel that way after I tell you about the news Aiden gave me today," he said. Corbin took the pot she was drying from her and the towel. "I'll finish the last of these up and you pour us some wine. I think you'll need it for this conversation."

"Well, shit," she mumbled. Corbin finished up the few dishes she had washed, drying them and putting them away. Ava had poured them both some wine and was waiting for him at the center island. He could tell that her worry had amped up and he again wished they didn't have to discuss what Aiden had learned about her father, but there was no getting around the news. He just needed to get it out and be by her side while she processed everything.

"Your father was the one driving the car the night of Ash's accident," he blurted out. Ava sat her wine glass down so hard, he worried that she broke it.

"What?" she asked. "How is that possible? He was in D.C. the time of the accident. I remember the police showing up to my house that night. It was just me and the nanny until my Grandpa showed up."

"I don't know all the details yet, but Aiden found two of the fraternity brothers who were at the party that night. Your grandfather was never called about Ashton. In fact, they said your father showed up and insisted that your brother leave with him. Made a big show of taking his keys away from him, saying he'd drive."

"So, Ash is really innocent?" Why would he willingly turn himself into the police for a crime he didn't commit?" That was a very good question and one that he had been mulling over all day.

"All I can come up with is that Ashton believes that he did it. Why else would he have run and then showed up all these years later to turn himself in. Someone told your brother that he hit and killed that woman," Corbin said.

"And, he's lived with that guilt all these years," Ava whispered. "We've got to get him out of that place," she insisted. This was what Corbin was most afraid of. He worried that telling Ava the news would spark a fire in her and she'd go off half-crazy and do something dangerous.

"We will, honey," he promised. "But, you have to let Aiden and I handle this. He's got the resources we need to get to your father and we need to let them play out."

"But, if we could just get him to confess," she interrupted.

"No," Corbin barked.

"But—" Ava tried to protest but he covered her mouth with his hand.

"I said no," Corbin growled. "You will not try to see your father to get a confession out of him. If he finds out that we know the truth, he'll do whatever it takes to stop you from telling the world." Corbin hesitantly removed his hand from her pouty lips when she nodded her head. "He let your brother go to prison for a crime that he didn't commit. What do you think he'd do to you if he found out that you know the truth?"

Ava sighed, "You're right," she grumbled.

"Tell me you'll let Aiden and I handle this," he insisted.

"I promise," she said, holding up her right hand as if swearing an oath.

"Good girl," he praised. "I'll get the door," he offered when the doorbell sounded. "Our food is here." Ava squealed and pulled some plates and forks from the cupboards. Corbin knew that the distraction of food would only last so long and Ava would be back on the hunt to find the truth. It was just who she was, promise or no promise, his girl was probably going to stick her nose in where it didn't belong and he just hoped like hell he'd be there to keep her safe.

AVALON

Ava sat in her car in front of her father's house. She had
done the exact opposite of what Corbin asked her to do
and snuck away to confront her dad. She had basically
fulfilled her end of the bargain she made with Corbin a
few weeks prior, but she was done waiting. Ava gave
Aiden and Corbin time to come up with answers and
they still had nothing but theories to go on. Time was
running out for her brother and she had to do something—for Ash's sake. So, Ava ditched her guard and
convinced Zara to help her come up with a plan to
record her conversation with her father. She'd do it all
again if it meant saving her brother from that God
awful place, even if it meant pissing off her husband.
She had been in to see Ashton every day in the last three
weeks he had been in that prison, and each time, he
looked worse. He went in strong and capable and now;
she saw him as a broken shell of a man who might not
make it back out of that place alive. Ava hadn't told him
about what Aiden found either. She couldn't give

Ashton hope, not while he was locked away. It wasn't fair to build him up for something that might not possibly happen.

"Stop being a chicken," she whispered to herself, looking at the big stone house that stoically stared back at her. She wondered if Zara was listening on the other end. They had done a few mic checks before she left, but that was no guarantee that her best friend could still hear her. Zara had reluctantly promised not to tell Aiden or Corbin where she was going or what she was up to. She also warned that if things went south, she'd be calling in the cavalry as back up and that would mean being found by one very angry husband.

Coming up with a plan to ditch her security wasn't easy but she did. Telling them that she had a doctor's appointment wasn't a stretch. She had one scheduled for that afternoon. Her personal guard told her that it would be no problem to accompany her to her appointment and he'd be happy to pick her up from work and take her. When Ava filled him in on the fact that she was seeing her OBGYN because she suspected she was pregnant, his expression was priceless. His face turned the cutest shade of red and the way he stood in front of her, rendered speechless by her news, was a perfect distraction. He agreed to not only keep her secret from her husband, claiming she wanted to surprise him, but he told her that it would be perfectly fine for her to go to her "girly doctor" by herself and to just check in when she was done. That was something she could do and hopefully, she and Corbin would have more than just news of a baby to celebrate tonight. She wanted to be able to share her good news with her brother too, but Ava wanted to wait until he was free from prison to do it. If today went well, she'd be celebrating two things tonight. Sure, Corbin would spank her ass bright red for defying him yet again, but what choice did she have? Ashton was her brother and she couldn't let her father get away with his lie for another day longer.

"Here goes nothing," she whispered to herself. Ava opened her car door and walked up the path to the big, red front door. Her mother had painted that door red, much to her father's protest and it was the only thing from her mom still left in place. When he'd have it repainted, she'd hold her breath as if worried he would choose a different color, but he always had it done bright red, just as her mom chose.

Her father pulled the door open before she could even raise her hand to knock. "Avalon," he hissed.

"Dad," she coldly returned. "I think we need to talk." Her father poked his head out the front door and looked around as if he expected to find her entourage that usually accompanied her, at Corbin's insistence.

"I see you left your Neanderthal husband and guards at home," he said. Ava nodded and he grabbed her arm and pulled her into the front foyer, slamming the door shut behind her. "Now," he said. "This is so much better. We can talk in private and not air our differences out in public. I take it you're here about my lawyer's questions?" he asked.

Ava smirked at him and shook her head. His team of lawyers had been hounding both her and Corbin since she told her father they were married. He made it his personal business to poke at their marriage and she almost wanted to laugh at the irony. Her father would never allow anyone poking their noses into his business and now she knew why—they'd find his skeletons.

"No, Dad," she said. "I'm here because I wanted to tell you about some information that I've come across that might help Ashton's case," she said. She knew she was teasing him, only feeding him small bits of information, but she couldn't help herself. Ava almost felt like savoring this moment. "Not that you've seemed overly concerned about your son, since he's been back."

"That boy has been nothing but trouble," he hissed. "He did the crime, now he can serve his time. This family has a long, proud lineage of men who did the right thing. I'm sure they would all be ashamed of what Ashton has done to the Michaels name," her father said.

Again, Ava had to refrain from laughing in his smug face. "Did you know Ash was alive this whole time?" she questioned.

Her father shrugged, as if it wasn't a big deal and she had her answer. "I assumed he wasn't dead," he offered. "You were the one who conjured up that story."

"Because it was easier than the truth. I was a little girl whose mother died and her brother took off. It was easier to think he died rather than believe that he didn't want to be around us." Ava bit the side of her cheeks, trying to stop her threatening tears. The last thing she wanted was to give him the satisfaction of seeing her cry.

"Well, that was on you. I had nothing to do with your overly active imagination," he said.

"But, you did have something to do with Ashton leaving, didn't you Dad?" She knew she was rushing the point but it was time for this show to begin.

"Just what are you hinting at, Avalon?" he asked. Her father crossed his arms over his chest, just as he used to do when she was a kid and she knew she was in trouble. Seeing him do this now only made her want to burst into fits of giggles.

"Nothing, really," she lied. "I've just started running with a very different circle of friends lately, Daddy. They've had some things to tell me about the night that Ash disappeared, although I'm not sure you'd be surprise by most of it."

Her father waved his hand through the air. "People gossip especially about men like me," he offered as an excuse.

"Men like you?" Ava questioned.

"Sure. Rich, powerful men," he said. "Always trying to bring us down but only the weak fall, Avalon. I taught you that." He had taught her that but now, she was going to be able to prove him wrong. Ava took great satisfaction knowing that she was going to be the one to topple her father's empire, once and for all.

"You sure about that, Dad?" she taunted. "They were two of the guys at the fraternity party, where you found Ashton that night." Ava could see the panic behind his eyes. Her father's smile was easy but his eyes always gave him away.

"Absolutely," he said. "Besides, who would believe some fraternity boys instead of me—a former Senator?"

"I don't know, Dad, they were pretty convincing,"

she said. "They did grow up, you know. Those fraternity boys are now a prize winning journalist with a national television syndicate and a decorated police detective who also happens to be a veteran. I'm thinking that the two of them combined trump a former Senator."

Her father barked out his laugh and Ava knew she had him right where she wanted him. It was his tell, his nervous tick and all she had to do now was reel him in. "What exactly are these frat boys saying about me, Ava?" he questioned.

She knew her smile was mean; she could feel it. "Oh, just that you showed up to the party that night and had an argument with Ash. You forced him to give you his keys and leave with you. And, my favorite part—you were the one driving that night. You hit that woman, didn't you, Daddy? You were the one who left her for dead in the middle of that road, not Ash." Ava felt as if she had run a marathon, lobbing accusations at her father but she didn't stop.

"You can't prove that—no one can," he spat. "You and your brother never understood all of the sacrifices I made for you." Ava wanted to laugh at just how untrue that was. Her father never did one unselfish thing in his life.

"Please, tell me how unselfish you are, Dad. What exactly did you do for us? Ash is in jail now because of something you did." She knew she was pushing but she was running out of time. If she didn't get her father to say the words and admit what he did, she might never be able to prove her brother's innocence.

"Ash was collateral damage," he said. "Just like you

will be, Avalon." Her father pulled a gun from his jacket pocket and pointed it at her. Ava made a move for the door but he shouted for her to stop and she had no choice. Her father would have shot her. He had all but proven that he didn't give a shit about her or Ashton.

Ava turned to face him and she could see the determination in his eyes. "You can't just shoot me, Dad," she said. "How will you cover that up? It won't be so easy this time. People know where I am. They know the truth."

"Who knows, Avalon? Your husband and some former frat boys?" he asked.

"Sure," she said. "Them and the new Senator who won Grandpa's seat. Aiden and a few of his friends on the police force know. In fact, they're on their way here now," she lied. "It's over, Dad."

"Why did you have to go and stick your nose into this, Ava? It didn't have to end like this," her father said. He almost looked upset about having to kill her —almost.

"So, how's this going to end, Dad?" she asked, not hiding her bitter tone. "You are just going to shoot me and then what? Bury me in the backyard under Mom's rose bushes?"

He chuckled, "Don't be silly, Avalon. I got rid of your mother's rose bushes a long time ago," he taunted. "I thought we could sit down and write a suicide note and then you could swallow a bottle of pills. Not too messy that way and I'm sure a whole lot less painful. You can just fall asleep and forget this whole ugly mess."

"I won't," she choked. "I think I'm pregnant and I

won't do that to my child. You might be a monster who can do that kind of thing to your kids but I'm not."

"Really, Avalon," he said. His tone was dry and condescending and she knew he didn't care if she was carrying his grandchild or not. "I would be doing the world a favor. Anything that you and that caveman husband of yours created won't be an asset to our family."

"At least tell me what really happened that night," she pleaded. Ava knew that if Zara was listening, keeping her father talking might be her only plan for staying alive. She would have called in the cavalry by now, or at least that was what Ava had hoped.

"I'm not sure what you want from me, Ava. Do you want me to admit my guilt and profess my deep sorrow for what I had done? That woman practically jumped out in front of that fucking car and there was no way for me to avoid her. I knew she was dead as soon as I saw her lying in the middle of the road. Your dumb ass brother had passed out as soon as we left the party, so he had no clue as to what had just happened." Her father's laugh was mean.

"You ran that poor woman down and left her for dead," she sobbed. "And, then you pinned it all on Ash. He was just a kid and you let him take the fall for what you did."

"He wasn't a kid. He acted like a fucking kid but he was a grown man. He should have acted more responsibly. If he was more like me and less like your mother, none of this would have happened. I would have never found your brother at that party, drunk and trying to drag our family's name through the mud. He would have destroyed my political career if he wasn't stopped. I just turned the circumstances around and took care of two problems. I had a dead woman on my hands and your brother needed to grow the hell up and stop all of his partying."

"So, you dumped him off at Grandpa's? Did he help you? Was my grandfather a part of your scheme?" she asked. Ava wasn't sure if she wanted to know the answer but she had no other way around it. She had put her grandfather up on a metaphorical pedestal and she worried that she was wrong about the man who she loved so very much.

"No," her father breathed. "My father would have never helped me. He would have protected Ashton with his life and he did. He kept Ash's secret and sent him away rather than watch his grandson face jail time. He protected you both."

"That's how you got him to put my marriage clause in his will, isn't it?" Ava asked. "You blackmailed him."

"Very good," her father praised. "Look at you figuring things out." She hated that he was smugly taunting her but she had no choice but to play along. "I told him that I found out about what Ashton had done. I threatened to use my money and resources to find Ash and drag him home to face his punishment, if he didn't put that clause into place. He knew I'd do it too, so he agreed. But, you found your way past that clause, didn't you, Avalon?"

He was right, she had, and thinking about Corbin now made her regret going against his orders and running to confront her father. If she had just obeyed him, none of this would be happening and she would be safely at work. Ava had to remember that she was doing all of this for Ashton, though. Her brother never had anyone besides her grandfather in his corner. Now that her Grandpa was gone, sticking up for Ash was her responsibility and one she didn't take lightly.

"Sorry I went and found the man of my dreams and fell in love, Dad," she sassed.

"You fucked everything up, Ava. My father's money should have been mine, but he chose to give it to you—a spoiled brat who didn't deserve it."

"You have more money than you should have been able to spend in your lifetime," she yelled. "But, you managed to do just that, didn't you Dad? You lost it all and now, you want what is mine. That was your plan all along, right?"

"No, but I have to admit, things did work out pretty perfectly. I couldn't have planned it any better—well, until you went and got married. I guess we can call that decision the beginning of your end," he said.

"You still haven't told me how you convinced Ashton that he was guilty of hit and run," she said, trying to buy more time.

"Like I said earlier, he passed out and missed all the excitement. I drove back here and moved him to the driver seat, with the keys still in the ignition. I took my jet and flew to Washington, D.C. and even paid off my maid to back my story of being in the Capital the whole time, if it came down to that. Your brother woke up and found the damaged front end of his car and put two and two together himself, after the news broke of the hit and run accident, leaving that woman dead. It was almost too easy with the way he stitched it all together for me. I didn't have to lift a finger and your grandfather stepping in, to keep Ashton out of prison, was the icing on the cake. All I had to do was sit back and wait for it all to happen." Her father looked almost proud of himself. He destroyed their whole family and stood there to boast about it?

"You're a monster," she shouted.

"Maybe," he agreed. "But the good news is you won't have to deal with me for much longer. Let's go on up to your mother's old sitting room. That might be a fitting place for you to take your last breath, since it was where she took her own."

"No," Ava protested. "You won't get away with any of this," she insisted.

"Oh, Ava," he said. She hated the way he looked like he pitied her. "I already have." He walked towards her, pushing the gun into her side and she sobbed. "Move, Ava," he demanded. "Upstairs." Ava wasn't sure what other options she had. She turned to walk up the grand staircase, feeling the gun barrel in her back with every step.

"You could just let me go," she begged. "I won't tell anyone about this."

"Sorry Ava, but your word isn't good with me. Not anymore," he said. She was to the top step when his front door swung open, Corbin and Aiden stood on the other side.

"Corbin," Ava screamed. Her only thought was to

warn her husband. "He's got a gun." Her father spun around on the second to last step, training his gun on Corbin and she did the only thing she could think of. Ava pushed him in the back as hard as she could, hoping that it would be enough to make him lose his balance.

Her father looked back over his shoulder, as if trying to figure out just what had happened and before he started falling forward, he fired the gun. It was as if her entire world suddenly started moving in slow motion and all she could do was watch her father falling down the staircase.

"Ava," Corbin yelled, but she didn't look at him, worried that he wasn't really there. At some point, he had started up the stairs to her and before she could even take a breath, he had her wrapped in his arms. "Tell me you're alright, honey," he whispered into her ear.

"You're here?" she said, still too afraid to let herself hope.

"I'm here," he confirmed. "You got him, Aiden?" Corbin yelled down the stairs and it echoed throughout the foyer.

"Yeah, but he's in pretty rough shape," Aiden said. "He's knocked out cold and it looks like he broke his leg in the fall. The paramedics are about five minutes out. You're girl good?"

"I'm not sure," Corbin said. "Open your eyes and look at me, baby," he commanded. Ava squinted one eye open and Corbin laughed. "That's a start at least," he teased. "I need for you to tell me you're okay," he demanded.

Ava took a step back from him and looked herself up and down, as if accessing her current situation. Was she alright? That was a good question. Ava wasn't sure she'd ever be okay again, not after she found out just what kind of person her father was—what he was capable of.

"I—I think I am," she stuttered. "He shot you?" she asked. She heard the gun go off and worried that her father had shot Corbin, in his fall.

"Naw," Corbin drawled. "He shot at me, Darlin'," he said. "Thank fuck your father has awful aim. I'm sure it didn't hurt that he was tumbling down a flight of steps at the time.

"How did you know where I'd be?" she questioned. Honestly, her brain felt as if it wasn't all caught up yet.

"You mean after you went behind my back and against my wishes to sneak over here?" He asked. Ava shrugged and Corbin cocked his eyebrow at her which was never a good sign. That usually meant that he was going to wait her out for her answer, but not believe a word that came out of her mouth anyway. That look usually landed her bare-assed, over his lap, getting her ass spanked red.

"I just couldn't sit by and not do anything, Corbin. Ashton is my brother and seeing him day in and day out, rotting away in that awful place—I just couldn't take anymore. I had no other choice," she said.

"Yeah, you did, honey. You could have trusted that Aiden and I were working on things on our end. I told you that I'd have your and your brother's backs and I meant it. Instead of obeying me, you just went out on your own and almost got yourself killed." Corbin stroked his big hand down his beard and she could tell that she had completely stressed him out. It was his tell tale sign that he was at his wits end and she was responsible for driving her poor husband there this time.

"I'm sorry," she whispered. "You're right."

"Damn straight, I'm right," he growled. "Thank God Zara had the good sense to tell Aiden about your crazy ass plan. Really, honey—you wore a wire?" Ava shrugged again. She seemed to be doing a lot of that since Corbin showed up to save her ass.

"Zara told you where to find me?" she asked.

"She did one better than just tell me where I'd be able to find my wife. She gave me the bug you wore, so I could hear exactly what was going on here while I was driving," Corbin said. Ava cringed at the idea that Corbin heard every sorted detail, including the part where she thought she was pregnant. It wasn't the way she wanted to tell him, but from the beautiful, furious frown he wore, he had heard it all.

"Was the part about you being pregnant a lie to throw your father off, honey?" he whispered. Ava shook her head, too overcome to find her voice.

"Say something," she begged. "Anything, Corbin. Just please don't be mad at me because I'm not sure if I'm pregnant and if I am, I don't want you to be upset."

CORBIN

"Upset?" he asked. "Why the hell would I be upset about a baby?" He wouldn't be either. The thought of Avalon pregnant with his child did crazy things to his heart.

"Because you don't seem happy," she said.

"I'm not happy about the rest of this," he said, wildly waving his arms around, as if trying to prove his point. "Do you have any idea how crazy it made me to hear your father talk about his plan to kill you? If anything would have happened to you, honey—" Corbin's voice broke and he hated showing any weakness around Ava. He wanted to be her rock, her solitude and the person she knew she could turn to for anything. But, she was his weakness. Ava was the only thing that could break him and losing her would have left him broken.

"I'm still here, Corbin," she said. "You haven't lost me."

"But, I almost did," he growled. "When Zara admitted what you two were up to, Aiden and I left the office immediately. Do you know what I went through when I heard that your father had a gun pointed at you?" His voice cracked again with emotion and Ava reached for him, but he couldn't let her touch him. He'd never get the rest out if he did.

He hated feeling so completely out of control and not being there to protect his wife made him feel exactly that way. "You ditched your guards," he shouted. "Did you even have a doctor's appointment today?"

"Yes," she whispered. "At two."

"And when were you fucking going to tell me about the possibility of a baby?" he yelled.

Ava jumped, startled by his question. "I was going to surprise you, Corbin," she whispered.

"The EMT's are here, guys. How about you take this down a notch? I'll handle everything down here," Aiden said.

"Thanks, man." Corbin nodded.

"I have a feeling the police are going to want to talk to Ava, too," Aiden finished.

"That's fine," Corbin said. "I'm done talking for now. I can't do this anymore, honey. I need some time to think things through." He turned and walked down the steps and all Ava could do was watch him leave. Corbin disappeared out the big, red front door and the last thing he saw was his best friend's disappointment, as he passed Aiden on his way out.

It had been five hours since he walked away from Ava. Well, five hours, thirteen minutes and forty-two seconds, to be exact, but who was counting? In that time, Zara had tried to call him twelve times and Aiden, four. Even his mother called a few times and when he texted that he was fine but wanted some space, Rose told him to stop being a fucking baby and deal with his shit like a grown-up. He had to admit, his mother's messages were the bright spot in his whole fucking day and who knew, maybe she was right. But up until about thirteen minutes ago, he wasn't ready to deal with any of this mess and sulking felt like his best option. So, he locked himself away in his office and ignored the constant texts, phone calls and his mother's persistent, annoying nagging through his door.

Thirteen minutes ago, the entire universe changed and he realized that if he didn't take his mother's advice, he'd lose the best thing in his life. Technically, the best two things, given the news Ava had sent him via text. It was time for him to get over the possibility of losing his wife and move forward with his plan to keep her. He acted like an ass; he panicked and now, he hoped like hell his wife would forgive him.

Where are you? Corbin texted her after receiving a picture of the sonogram of their baby. He missed his kid's first milestone and he hated that. He had a father who missed everything and he wouldn't be anything like his dad. He owed it to this kid to be more for him or her.

Home. Ava texted back. He packed up his briefcase and made a beeline for the elevator, ignoring his mother's pleas for him to stop. His only thought was getting home to his wife and groveling for forgiveness.

216

"Sorry, Ma," he said. "Got to go and beg my wife to forgive me for being an ass." The elevator doors closed but the last thing he saw was his mother's triumphant, goofy grin.

He sped home, not wanting to waste a minute and when he got to the penthouse, he worried that he wouldn't find Ava still there. His panic gave way when he found her soaking in a bubble bath in the master bedroom. She was completely covered in bubbles, just her head sticking out of the water, her eyes closed.

"Hey," he breathed. Ava peeped one eye open and quickly closed it again. "I'm sorry," he whispered.

"For?" she asked. He wanted to laugh, but judging from her icy reception, she wasn't in the mood to find anything he said funny.

"You aren't going to make this easy on me, are you, honey?" he teased. She opened her eyes and looked at him and Corbin wished he hadn't just said what he did.

"This isn't a joke, Corbin," she said. "I had to go to our baby's first doctor visit alone. I had to face the police alone and I had to deal with everything my father told me—alone."

"In all fairness, Ava," he said, sitting on the edge of the tub, "you did go off this morning to face your father, alone. You were going to go to the doctor by yourself and I'm pretty sure that if you didn't get Zara in on your crazy plan, you would have died today—alone," his voice broke and he knew that he needed to calm the fuck down. The last time they had a shouting match, he ended up walking away from the only woman he had ever loved.

"I know that, Corbin. That's why I'm mad at myself, not you. I'm the one who should be telling you how sorry I am." Ava stood from the tub, the soapy bubbles running down her body and he didn't hesitate to pull her into his arms. "I'm all wet," she complained.

"Mmm, that's my favorite way for you to be, honey," he teased. "How about we both agree to forgive the other and move forward from there?" he asked.

"How do we move forward, Corbin?" she asked.

That was something he had given a lot of thought to over the past few hours. "We have to trash all of our old rules and just have one new rule between the two of us."

"Trash the rules?" Ava said. "But, why?"

"Because you aren't my submissive anymore, Ava. You're more than that now—you're my wife. When this thing started out between the two of us, I planned on making you mine slowly. What started out as you being my reluctant submissive ended up with me falling madly in love with you." Ava framed his face with her wet hands. "I feel the same way, Corbin. But, I need your dominance. I'm not sure that this thing works between the two of us without it," she whispered.

"Thank fuck, honey," he growled. "Because, I have no idea how to be anything but dominant with you. How about our one rule be that we are just completely honest with each other from here on out?" Ava pretended to weigh her pros and cons and he swatted her bare, wet ass, causing her to yelp.

"Okay," she said. "Complete honesty. But, I think we need to amend your one rule policy."

"How's that?" he asked.

Ava smiled at him and it nearly took his breath away, she was so fucking beautiful. "All your prior rules stand and we add the honesty one to the mix." He palmed her ass and she wiggled against his body.

"I think you just like having the extra rules in place so you have more chances of breaking them," he said. Her giggle told him he was right on track.

"Well, I do like when you spank me," she sassed. "Do you think you can handle that?" she asked.

"I think I can work with the rules, Mrs. Eklund," he said.

"That's good to hear, Mr. Eklund because I've broken a few of them just today," she teased.

"Well then, Wife, I think it's time for me to take you off to our bed and spank your ass a pretty shade of pink."

Ava squealed and clapped her hands together and he hauled her over his shoulder, carrying her to their room. Corbin felt like the luckiest man on earth, holding his entire future against his body and he wasn't sure how he deserved such a perfect submissive, but Ava was his and that was all that mattered.

EPILOGUE

AVALON

Three Months Later

Ava waited for Corbin at her office and she was starting to get a little edgy. Being five months pregnant really didn't lend to her patience and it wasn't her strong suit to begin with. She paced the front lobby like a lioness watching for her prey, keeping an eye out for Corbin's black SUV.

"Hey beautiful," he said, startling her from behind.

"Corbin," she screeched. "You scared the shit out of me."

"Language," he said, covering her barely there baby bump. This was the first week that she was beginning to look like she was pregnant and he was having trouble keeping his hands to himself. "We don't want his first words being a curse word."

"I'm sure it won't be and what if it's a she?" Ava reached down to put her hands over his, loving being able to share this new experience with Corbin.

Corbin palmed her belly and smiled. "I'm sure she will be the best first girl quarterback on her high school football team," he teased.

"Or a ballerina," Ava quickly added.

"Sure," Corbin said. "Although, she'll look silly hiking the ball in a tutu." Ava giggled and Corbin pulled her in for a quick kiss. "Ready?" he asked. "I had my driver park around the back. Traffic is crazy tonight."

"Are you going to tell me where we are going and what all this secrecy is about?" Corbin told her to be ready to leave work at five on the dot because he had something he wanted to show her. Her husband forgot the fact that she really hated surprises or secrets and when she begged him to give her a hint, he reminded her who was in charge. Ava knew he was distracting her but she had to admit, he was pretty good at the art of diversion.

"We will be there in less than ten minutes, but if you can't be patient and behave, Wife, I'm sure I can get our driver to circle around town while I remind you how to be a good girl." Corbin's devilish grin made her girl parts want his undivided attention and she was always up for car sex, but Ava was too curious to give in to her overly active libido.

"Fine," she said. "I'll play nice." Ava pouted and took his hand, following him out to his waiting car.

"You only have to play nice for a few minutes, honey.

And then, you can play as dirty as you'd like." His words dripped with innuendo and it took all of Ava's will power not to ask him to make good on his promise to punish her in the back of his car.

The ride felt like it took forever and the touching and kissing didn't seem to help her body to cool down any. Ava just hoped that whatever it was he wanted to show her didn't take long. She was anxious to get back to their penthouse and show Corbin just how dirty she liked to play.

The car pulled up in front of the club where she and Corbin met, to spend their very first night together. "Um, I thought we couldn't come here anymore because you were worried about our privacy?" she asked. After her father went to prison, Ava hoped that Corbin would want to take her back to her favorite BDSM club but he told her that they wouldn't have any privacy there. They had gone to France a few times since and played at his club there but she wondered if they'd ever find a place to play in the States.

"I was worried about our privacy," he agreed. "That's why I bought this place and renamed it." Corbin pointed up to a giant black sign with red letters that spelled out her name.

"Avalon," she read her name and smiled. "You named your new BDSM club after me?" Ava wasn't sure if that was the weirdest or sweetest thing she had ever heard.

"Yep," he proudly said. "You okay with all of this?"

Honestly, Ava was more than just alright with Corbin owning the club—she was ecstatic. This hopefully meant they would be able to go out to play and that idea had her body's need amping up to new levels. "Does this mean we can play?" she questioned.

"I'd like to, but only if your ready for this. I know that some of your father's old friends might be in there from time to time. Hell, Aiden and Zara might even come over to play. You have to know that we will not have the same privacy we do when we go to play at my club in France. You good with that?"

Ava wrinkled up her nose at the thought of seeing Zara and Aiden at the club. She knew her friend and her husband liked kink but that was something she didn't want to see. "How about on nights when it's less private, we go back to our own room?" she asked. "I'm not sure that seeing Aiden and Zara playing at the club is something I'm looking forward to. Can we keep your private room for ourselves—as a secret retreat? We'll just have to work out a schedule."

"Sure," Corbin offered. "I think that sounds fair."

"Besides," she said, knowing this next part might just piss him off. "Your mother might show up one night to play and then you'll want to hide away in our private room."

"No," Corbin growled pointing his finger at her. "Take that back," he ordered.

"Oh, come on, Corbin. You have to know that Rose is into kink. You didn't invent it," she teased.

"It's just not going to happen," he insisted. "Ever," he added. "I don't want to talk about my mother anymore. How about I take you into our new club and show you one more surprise I got for you."

"Another surprise?" she asked. "Wow, I must have been a very good girl," she teased.

"You have and I've checked with your doctor and we are clear to play." Corbin wagged his eyebrows at her and she giggled. Ava loved how protective Corbin was with their baby already. She knew that he would take extra precautions to keep both her and the baby safe but calling her doctor was the sweetest.

"Well then, show me your club," she said.

"Our club," he corrected. "You remember your safe word?" he asked.

"Yep—ice cream," she said.

"Good girl," he praised. "Let's play."

Corbin had remodeled the playroom and his special surprise for her was a Saint Andrew's cross that Ava couldn't wait to use. "It's beautiful," she gushed. "All of it, Sir."

"I'm glad you like it," Corbin whispered against her ear. "Now strip and get your ass over to that cross." She did just as he ordered, loving the way he never took his eyes off her. He helped Ava up against the cross and made sure that the wood wasn't touching her belly. He secured her ankles and wrists to the beams, leaving her spread eagle, her front to the wood, gifting him with a glorious view of her ass.

He gave her ass a smack, "This is mine," he growled.

"Yes, Sir," she agreed. "Everything I have is yours."

Ava could feel his possessiveness in his every touch, as he let his big hands glide down her bare body.

Corbin walked around to the back of the cross to stand in front of her and smirked. He held up a flogger in one hand, with what looked to be a soft leather tip and a leather paddle in the other. The paddle looked like something that, if used properly, could leave a mark. "Well," he challenged. "Which one would my wife like for me to use tonight?" he asked.

"I get to pick?" she questioned.

Corbin shrugged, "This is for your pleasure tonight, so sure," he agreed. Ava smiled at the possibilities but suddenly felt very unsure of which to choose. "Tick-tock," he pushed.

"Um, the paddle?" she said. It sounded more like a question than an answer and Corbin chuckled.

"You asking or telling me, baby?" he teased.

"Telling," she said with a nod of her head. "The paddle."

"You do like a little bit of a bite, don't you, honey?" he asked. He ran the soft leather of the flogger down her body and lightly tapped her already wet pussy with the pad. Her husband knew just what his little show was doing to her but he wanted to see for himself, firsthand. He raised the flogger back up to inspect it and hummed his approval.

"You're so fucking ready, aren't you, Ava?" he asked.

"Yes Sir," she agreed.

"Then let's get this show started. Once I'm done working your ass over, I'm going to take you like this.

Do you like the idea of being bound to the cross while I'm fucking you from behind, Ava?"

"Yes," she hissed. Corbin landed a hard slap on her ass with the paddle and she yelped.

"Yes?" he questioned.

"Yes, Sir," she corrected.

"Better," he praised. "Count for me, Avalon," he ordered. She loved to be spanked, but when it was for her pleasure and not a punishment, Corbin always played with her a little more. Tonight was no different. He dipped his fingers through her folds and back, using the paddle to spank her ass. Avalon kept count and when he got to twenty, she felt as though she could literally fly. She loved this feeling—Corbin called it subspace, but it felt more like heaven. Ava never wanted to come back down once she got there.

At some point, she must have stopped counting because every time the paddle met one of her fleshy globes, Corbin growled out the number they were on. "Twenty-five," he hoarsely shouted. Corbin tossed the paddle to the side of the cross and she could hear him lower his zipper. He was behind her, filling her and rubbing up against her raw skin from the spankings and it was almost too much for her. Ava cried out his name when she was close, and Corbin picked up the pace, pumping in and out of her body.

He snaked his arms around her, sealing himself up against her backside, reaching around to palm her sensitive nipples and just that extra friction was all she needed. Ava soared and Corbin followed her over, whispering praises of love into her ear as he helped her down from the cross. "Beautiful," he praised. "You are so fucking beautiful, Ava."

"I'm yours, Sir," she whispered. "I'm still your submissive, right?"

"Yes," he agreed. "You are so much more than that though, my wife. You are my reluctant submissive and you are mine."

ROSE

Rose Eklund sat at the end of the large mahogany bar and tossed back her shot of vodka. She usually didn't drink the hard stuff, but if she had to celebrate her fiftieth birthday, she'd do it in epic proportions. At least she figured that the hangover she was sure to have tomorrow would be pretty damn epic. She might be another year older but that didn't mean she had to slip into her new year quietly or willingly. She was going to go down fighting and angry as piss about turning a half a century old.

Her son, Corbin, had offered to throw her a party but that was the very last thing she wanted. As far as she was concerned, fifty could come in quietly and no one had to be the wiser. Then, come morning, she was going to march right into her son and his best friend's offices and announce that she was retiring. Sure, it was a little early but why not? Rose had spent her entire life taking care of everyone else and it was time for her to take care of herself for a change.

She had Corbin just shy of her seventeenth birthday and against her parents' wishes. They had begged her to terminate her pregnancy when she found out she was going to have a baby. Her son's father was almost ten years older than she was and when he found out she was expecting, he took off. Her parents had threatened to press charges and throw him in jail for getting a minor pregnant and he didn't bother to stick around and meet his kid.

Rose was forced to grow up quickly, out in the world on her own as a single mom. She had a baby who was depending on her and parents who wanted nothing to do with her. She moved into a little efficiency apartment and didn't once allow herself to wallow in self-pity—there just wasn't time for it. She got her GED, finishing up her senior year at night and working at a local convenience store during the day. She relied on the kindness of friends and neighbors to help watch Corbin and after she graduated and could get a better paying job, she decided to pay back the kindness that was shown to her any way she could.

When her ten-year-old son brought home a new friend from school, she instantly took a liking to Aiden Bentley. He was scrawny and shy and for the life of her, Rose couldn't figure out how the two had become friends. Her son was loud and outgoing and usually the biggest kid in his class but he and Aiden seemed to hit it off from the start. Aiden's mother left him when he was little and his father was a drunk who couldn't seem to get his shit together, even for his only son. So, when she saw that Aiden was struggling to get by, she stepped up and lent a hand. Before long, he was spending nights at her house and just about every waking minute too. He had practically moved in with her and Corbin and that was just fine with her. She considered him her son and she could tell he loved her like a mother.

When the boys went away to college, Rose panicked, worrying about what her next stage in life was going to be. She was only thirty-five years old and she wasn't quite sure what she was supposed to do with herself. She took a few college classes and got her AA degree in business management, which came in handy when the guys graduated from college and announced that they were opening their own company. Rose agreed to help out in her spare time and they jokingly called her their assistant. They set up shop in her basement and Rose felt more like a babysitter than an assistant, at first. But the guys seemed to really find their niche and grew the small start-up into a multi-million dollar company. She was proud of them and thankful that they kept her around.

She became Aiden's assistant and honestly, that worked for them all. She got to see her two favorite guys and Aiden's kids all she wanted and Rose was sure she couldn't be any happier. But turning fifty had thrown her for a loop and she wasn't sure which end was up. It was time for her to get off the ride and slow down some. She wanted to travel and explore the world while she was still somewhat young and it was about time she took a chance on life. She didn't want to wait another twenty birthdays to find out that she didn't really live her life and was too old to do anything about it.

"This one is from the gentleman at the other end of the bar," the bartender loudly whispered over the bad honky tonk music. Rose nodded to the handsome man who was facing her at the other end of the bar and swallowed back the shot of vodka, giving him a mock salute when she finished it.

He smiled at her and nodded, sipping his beer. He was probably younger than her, but most everyone in the bar was except the bartender and he wasn't her type. Rose wasn't much of a dater and the idea of being brazen enough to talk to a complete stranger at a bar made her nervous. Honestly, she could count on one hand the number of men she had been with since having Corbin and that was fine with her, really. She had a son to take care of and dating just never seemed a priority. When Corbin was a toddler, her best friend had tried to fix her up with a guy but he wasn't really interested in a twenty-year-old with a toddler in tow. Most guys weren't into single mothers at that age and Rose decided to save herself some heartache and time by deciding to stay out of the dating pool. Sure, she was lonely, but she had Corbin and Aiden and a whole drawer full of vibrators.

"Hi," a sexy, deep voice whispered into her ear. Rose turned to find the man who was formerly sitting at the end of the bar, now perched on the seat next to her. "I'm Clayton," he said, holding his hand out for her to shake. "But everyone calls me Clay."

"Um," she stuttered, cursing herself for having the

fourth shot. She knew her limit was three but when he sent her the drink, she didn't want to seem rude and refuse. "Rose," she said, placing her hand in his and gently shaking it.

"Nice to meet you, Rose," he said. She couldn't stop staring at him. He was definitely younger than she was and probably the most handsome man she had seen in some time. Honestly, he looked more like one of her son's friends than someone who'd be buying her drinks at a bar. His dirty blond hair was pushed back, as if he had been wearing a hat and had taken it off and his blue eyes matched the plaid blue shirt he was wearing. He reminded her of one of those cowboys she had seen in a western movie.

"Tell me you can ride a horse," she whispered. Rose wasn't sure she had even said those words out loud until he threw his head back and laughed at her. She smiled back but was really internally kicking herself for saying something so stupid.

"I can in fact ride a horse," he said. "It's kind of a prerequisite for owning a ranch." Rose nearly swallowed her tongue thinking about him fulfilling her dirty cowboy fantasies that she loved so much. They were honestly her favorite romance books to read—the ones with the sexy cowboys but meeting one in real life wasn't something she planned on.

"So what is a beautiful woman like you doing in a bar like this?" he asked.

Now it was Roses turn to laugh. "That is the cheesiest pick up line ever invented," she giggled.

"Well, I don't know about that," he drawled. "I got to

see that pretty smile of yours now, didn't I?" Rose wasn't sure if she successfully rolled her eyes, but she knew she was trying to.

"I'm here drowning my sorrows," she said.

"Please don't tell me that I'm going to have to find and beat the shit out of some asshole for breaking your heart, Rose," Clayton said.

"Oh God, no," Rose almost yelled. "No, no man or boyfriend to speak of," she said, holding up her hand and pointing to her empty ring finger. "It's my birthday," she said.

"Really?" Clay asked.

"Yep, and not a good one at that," she added. Rose sipped the water the bartender handed her and she nodded her thanks.

"What happened to make your day such a bad one?" Clay asked.

"I turned fifty," she admitted with a grimace.

"No fucking way," he said. Clay sounded almost as upset about her age as she felt.

"Fucking way," she said.

"Well, if it makes you feel any better, you don't look it," he said. As sweet as it was of him to say, it really didn't make her feel any better. Rose knew that she didn't look fifty and had good genes and night cream to thank for that, but she also didn't need anyone to blow smoke up her ass. She knew how old she was and there was nothing she could do about it.

"Thanks," she dryly said. "But it doesn't really soften the blow of that number."

"I get it," Clay said. "I'm here for the same reason."

"You're turning fifty today?" Rose questioned.

"Close—forty," Clay said.

Rose groaned and called the bartender back over. "I'll take a Moscow Mule and another beer for my ancient friend here," she teased.

"Hey," Clay complained.

"How about you come talk to me in another ten years and then you can properly complain about my slight," Rose teased.

"How about we help each other forget that we're turning another year older, Rose?" Clayton asked. Rose wasn't sure if the sexy stranger was asking her what she thought he was but she sure wanted to find out.

"Um, what?" she asked. Clayton smiled up at her and from the devilish grin he gave her, she was sure she had heard him correctly. The question was, would she be a coward and bail or finally do something she wanted and take him up on his offer?

CLAYTON

Clay had a shit day and since it was also his fortieth birthday, his obvious choice for ending his day was at his favorite bar. But tonight, instead of finding all the same prospects, he was happy to find a sexy little brunette in a business suit that made him completely hot and bothered. She was wearing sexy high heels that made him want to wrap her long legs around his neck and make her scream out his name. Even her name was pretty and Clay was sure that spending a night over or under her, for that matter, would help him forget about turning forty.

There was really no other way he would forget about his milestone birthday—his brother and business partner, Tyler, gave him a good deal of shit about being older and now that he was forty, his brother's propensity for making fun of him only seemed to grow. Of course it didn't help that his brother was younger than him by eight years. He was still a baby and Clay hated that he was starting to have trouble keeping up with him around their ranch. He didn't dare bitch about his back hurting or any of his new aches and pains otherwise, Ty would never let him live it down.

Now, he was sitting at his favorite bar in town, trying to forget the shit day he had by asking a pretty woman to spend the night with him. Sure, he was probably losing his mind and maybe even his grip on reality, but if he was going down, he wanted it to be with the sexy brunette who looked as though she could give just as good as she got.

"So, how about it, Rose?" he whispered close to her ear. He liked the way she shivered as his warm breath brushed over her skin. God, her skin looked soft. "Want to come home with me?" He asked. Rose gasped and turned an adorable shade of pink, making him chuckle. It was refreshing to meet a woman who seemed a little put-off by such an offer. Most of the women he met were usually pasted up against him by this point of the conversation and it was nice to know that women like Rose still existed.

"I appreciate your offer," she stammered. "But I don't think that would be a good idea. I'm a little older than you and we both know that come morning, you'll sober up and forget that you even met me tonight." She was wrong. Clay was only on his second beer and he was about ready to call it a night when he spotted Rose across the bar. Honestly, she looked about as sad and depressed as he felt and there would be no way he'd forget her.

"I hate to break it to you, but this here," he said, holding up his glass, "is my second beer. I'm not drunk, although I'd give my left nut to be. I'm alone and celebrating a milestone birthday, just like you. I thought we could commiserate together. And I can assure you honey, there would be no fucking way I'd be able to forget you, drunk or not," he admitted. Rose turned that adorable shade of red again and he was sure that he was going to be in a perpetual hard state if he didn't get her to agree to go back to his ranch with him.

"So, why are you here alone tonight?" Rose asked, not so subtly changing the subject. Clay could tell that she had a little more to drink than he had, but he was hoping that the waiter would bring her more water and less of those Moscow Mules she was drinking. If he was going to convince her to go home with him, he wanted her to be sober or as close to it as possible.

"I really didn't want to celebrate my birthday with anyone," he admitted. "I've never been one for big celebrations or blowing out candles to mark another passing year, so here I am." He held his arms wide as if trying to prove his point.

"What about your wife or girlfriend?" she pried.

He laughed, "Subtle," he teased. "Like you, I don't have either of those. I have a thirteen- year- old daughter but she is conveniently on vacation with her mother and new stepfather right now."

"That's awful," Rose said. "Your ex took her on vacation during your birthday?"

"Yep," he said. "It's fine really. What thirteen- year-old girl wants to hang out with her father for his fortieth birthday? My younger brother, Ty, offered to hang out with me tonight, but there was no way I wanted to spend my night hearing about how old I am from my thirty-two year old little brother."

"No," Rose agreed, sipping her water. "I think that would be an awful way to spend your birthday."

"Well, I can think of at least one way I'd like to spend both of our birthdays, but you would have to say yes," he said. He knew he was pushing a little and hell, maybe Rose thought he was a total creep but he really didn't care. He wanted a chance with her and if he had to beg for it that is exactly what he was going to do.

Rose sighed and he braced himself to be let down. "I want to," she admitted, surprising the hell out of him.

"Really?" Clay knew he sounded as surprised as he was but Rose had caught him off guard.

"Really," she confirmed. "But I have a list," she said.

"A list?" he questioned. "What kind of list are we talking here, Rose?" Clay asked. "Grocery, laundry, chores, demands?" He chuckled at his own joke but Rose seemed to find him a lot less funny.

"No, smart ass. A list of things I want and don't want in a man," she said.

Clay whistled his surprise, "So, it is a list of demands then," he said. "I'm guessing it's a long one?"

Rose rolled her eyes and nodded. "According to my son and well, his best friend, I'm a very picky dater. If you could call being out on five dates in the last thirty-three years dating at all."

Clay choked on his beer and set his bottle back on the bar. "You have only been out on five dates in thirty-three years? Shit, Rose," he said.

"Yeah," she whispered. "So, thanks for the offer but I

understand if you'd like to take it back now." Clay knew he had to play the rest of his hand smart otherwise he was going to spend the rest of his evening alone and the thought of having to watch Rose walk out of that bar and his life stung a little.

"What's number one?" he asked.

"Sorry," she said, seeming confused by his question.

"The first thing on your list of what you want and don't want in a man?" Clay asked. He knew he might be asking for trouble but he had to know. "If you're going to flat out reject me, I'd like to know the reason why."

"Um," Rose squeaked, "Number one would be the guy had to be older than me," she said. Her frown said it all and he knew that arguing would get him nowhere.

Clayton stood and laid down cash for both of their drinks. He nodded at Rose, "Thanks for your honesty," he said, tipping his hat to her. "At least you gave me that. Happy birthday, Rose." Clay turned to walk away and he was just about to the door when he felt a hand on his shoulder. He turned to find Rose looking up at him and the pleading look in her eyes nearly did him in. The country music was so loud that there would be no way he'd be able to hear anything she had to say. He could see her lips moving but that was about it. He pointed to his ear and shook his head, as if trying to signal to her that he couldn't hear her.

Clay could see her sigh even though he couldn't hear it. Rose went up on her tiptoes and wrapped her arms around his shoulders, taking him completely by surprise and gently brushed her lips against his. He wasn't sure if Rose was agreeing to everything that he wanted or just telling him goodbye, but either way he was going to take full advantage of having her pressed up against his body. Clay wrapped his arms around her and pulled her in closer loving the way she seemed to fit up against him and deepened their kiss. When she finally pulled free from him, she was panting and he could tell that he left her just as needy as she did him.

Rose smiled up at him and nodded and he was almost afraid to hope that she was giving her agreement for him to take her home. She didn't give him much time to think about anything, taking his hand into hers and yanking him along to the door. He followed her because honestly, the thought of going home alone sucked. If Rose was offering to spend their birthdays together, he'd make it one neither of them would ever forget—he deserved at least one happy fucking birthday.

The End
To be continued in Owned Book 3!

ABOUT K.L. RAMSEY

Romance Rebel fighting for Happily Ever After!

K. L. Ramsey currently resides in West Virginia (Go Mountaineers!). In her spare time, she likes to read romance novels, go to WVU football games and attend book club (aka-drink wine) with girlfriends.

K. L. enjoys writing Contemporary Romance, Erotic Romance, and Sexy Ménage! She loves to write strong, capable women and bossy, hot as hell alphas, who fall ass over tea kettle for them. And of course, her stories always have a happy ending.

K.L. RAMSEY'S SOCIAL MEDIA LINKS:

Facebook-> https://www.facebook.com/kl.ramsey.58
(OR) https://www.facebook.com/k.l.ramseyauthor/
Twitter-> https://twitter.com/KLRamsey5
Instagram -> https://www.instagram.com/itsprivate2/
Pinterest-> https://www.pinterest.com/klramsey6234/
Goodreads-> https://www.goodreads.com/author/show/17733274.K_L_Ramsey
Book Bub-> https://www.bookbub.com/profile/k-l-ramsey
Amazon.com-> https://www.amazon.com/K.L.-Ramsey/e/B0799P6JGJ/
Ramsey's Rebels-> https://www.facebook.com/groups/ramseysrebels/
Website-> https://klramsey.wixsite.com/mysite
KL Ramsey & BE Kelly's ARC Team-> https://www.facebook.com/groups/klramseyandbekellyarcteam
KL Ramsey & BE Kelly's Street Team-> https://www.facebook.com/groups/klramseyandbekellystreetteam
Newsletter->https://mailchi.mp/4e73ed1b04b9/authorklramsey

BE Kelly's social media links:

Instagram-> https://www.instagram.com/bekellyparanormalromanceauthor/
Facebook-> https://www.facebook.com/be.kelly.564
Twitter-> https://twitter.com/BEKelly9
Book bub-> https://www.bookbub.com/profile/be-kelly
Amazon->https://www.amazon.com/BE-Kelly/e/B081LLD38M
BE Kelly's Reader's group-> https://www.facebook.com/groups/530529814459269/

MORE WORKS BY K.L. RAMSEY

The Relinquished Series

Love Times Infinity

Love's Patient Journey

Love's Design

Love's Promise

Harvest Ridge Series

Worth the Wait

The Christmas Wedding

Line of Fire

Torn Devotion

Fighting for Justice

Last First Kiss Series

Theirs to Keep

Theirs to Love

Theirs to Have

Theirs to Take

Second Chance Summer Series

True North

The Wrong Mr. Right

Ties That Bind Series

Saving Valentine

Blurred Lines

Dirty Little Secrets

Taken Series

Double Bossed

Double Crossed

Owned

His Secret Submissive

His Reluctant Submissive

Coming Soon:

Alphas in Uniform

Hellfire

Royal Bastards MC

Savage Heat

Savage Hell MC Series

Roadkill

Works by BE Kelly (K.L.'s alter ego…)

Reckoning MC Seer Series

Reaper

Tank

Raven

Perdition MC Shifter Series

Ringer

Printed in Great Britain
by Amazon

40690097R00148